1 MONTH OF
FREE
READING

at

www.ForgottenBooks.com

By purchasing this book you are eligible for one month membership to ForgottenBooks.com, giving you unlimited access to our entire collection of over 1,000,000 titles via our web site and mobile apps.

To claim your free month visit:
www.forgottenbooks.com/free505656

ISBN 978-0-484-61523-5
PIBN 10505656

META'S FAITH.

BY

THE AUTHOR OF

" ST. OLAVE'S," " JANITA'S CROSS,"

" JEANIE'S QUIET LIFE,"

&c. &c.

"In our days, a man is the son of his own deeds."

IN THREE VOLUMES.

VOL. II.

LONDON:

HURST AND BLACKETT, PUBLISHERS,

13, GREAT MARLBOROUGH STREET.

1869.

The right of Translation is reserved.

LONDON:
PRINTED BY MACDONALD AND TUGWELL,
BLENHEIM HOUSE.

META'S FAITH.

CHAPTER I.

MEANWHILE Stephen Garton was working steadily on at his life plan, which was to secure a peaceful home for his mother in her old age, and to win for himself a place to work, and leave to work in this world. A plan which he would doubtless follow out as industriously as Mrs. Waldemar followed out hers; though not being largely gifted with that good lady's admirable tact and power of laying hold upon favourable circumstances, he might not win his way so rapidly to success.

Of those bright thoughts which gather round many a young man's future, making it warm and full of sunshine; thoughts of home, and the loved one whose presence makes that home, Stephen Garton had small store as yet. To strive, and to strive, and to strive; that had been the one command of life to him. Strife to which no bright eyes, no sweet woman smile impelled him, promising fair reward when all was done; but only Duty and Necessity, which cannot always drive a man so far as love's gentler influence can draw him. He knew nothing as yet of that happy inspiration which can carry a man on to almost any extent of effort so long as certain bright eyes—

" Rain influence and adjudge the prize."

One chamber, at any rate, in Stephen's heart was locked. Someone, somewhere in the wide world, might hold its key, and one day show all the treasures garnered there, but of that sweet perchance he had seldom time to think. Just to work patiently on was his duty, and he did it.

And lately there had been a new impulse to work.

This Burton prize was to be contested for in the coming autumn. Of the many who had entered their names on the Governor's books as competitors for it, only six remained. All the rest, discouraged by the severity of the study involved, had fallen away. Of the six, Stephen Garton was one.

The prize was of considerable value, independent of the honour which attached to the winning of it. It provided the successful competitor with the means of studying for three years at any of the German universities, or for a still longer period at the Carriden-Regis College. In addition to this, it greatly aided his progress in his profession, for the holder of the Burton medal had but to show it, and almost any position in his own denomination was open to him. He was made for life, for anyone with the slightest knowledge of scholarship knew that the amount of it which he must have gained to secure such a prize, would qualify him for a high stand amongst literary and culti- vated men.

It was for this that Stephen Garton was working so hard, for this that he spent so many lonely hours in that scantily-furnished little room of his, amongst the battered books and mean poverty-stamped surround- ings. He scarcely dared to dream as yet of the possibility of success. That he should ever be able to go to Germany and study at the world-renowned universities there; that he, the poor Millsmany weaver's son, should come into companionship with men whose very names were a sort of inspiration to him now, and that with the learning and experience gained from them, he should return to make for himself a fair name and reputation in the world, this was a dream almost too bright to be realised. It was too much like those fairy stories which the boys used to read by stealth at school, of invisible coats and magic helmets, and seven-leagued boots, wherewith the owners of them did such wondrous deeds of strength and heroism; deeds, alas! *only* done in story-books.

And yet, Stephen thought to himself, others had realized that dream before him. Neither prestige of birth nor influence was needed to win for a student all the honours that the Burton prize could give. Talent, patience, clear-thinking, steady resolve; only these, nothing more than these, had won it before, and would win it again. He knew he had them. It was not conceit. It was not an overweening estimate of his own powers that gave him courage to go on, but when he looked back and counted the steep rugged steps by which he had climbed from poverty and ignorance to his present fair platform of promise, he felt that so far as the mere struggle with circumstances was to be feared, the worst lay behind him. All that toil and endeavour, all that self-restraint and self-denial, had been helping to carve out a character which would not easily be daunted by difficulties, which would rather make use of those very difficulties as means whereby to raise itself to a higher level of enterprise.

And then, when those years of foreign study were over, and a fair field of honest

work lay before him; when he and grinding
poverty had shaken hands and bidden each
other farewell, and he could claim what every
man has a right to claim from the world
he labours in, a fair, equal price for that
labour, then the other, brighter visions which
had been floating in his mind, might shape
themselves into reality. He, too, so long
homeless, might have a home and a fireside
of his own, with some true woman to guard
them for him; a woman whose simple, peaceful nature should calm his own, so chafing
and restless; who should be to him what the
April sunshine was to these leaves and
flowers, what the evening dew is to the
thirsty grass which has withered for lack of
it all through the long sultry day. He could
live a noble life then. He knew he could.
He could so gladly toil and strive if only
her love strengthened him to the strife, if

only her smile was waiting for him when that strife was done.

Stephen had never seen such a woman, except in his dreams; but he believed that somewhere in the world she lived, and for her sake, whoever she might be, he kept his heart and life pure, so that one day they might clasp hands together, hers not stained by any touch of his.

Very different this, though, from the motive which held him to such long days and nights of study, and which made him deny himself almost the necessaries of life to find means for that study. That was his pride as a student and his duty as a son. He wanted to pay back the many years of care which that poor mother had spent over him. He wanted to make his very name a joy and a blessing to her. He wanted to show the world that he, the weaver's lad of Millsmany, had the make of a genuine worker in him, a worker who would leave his mark behind in the lives and memories of others.

He might have done all this, however, and been an untrue man still. He might have paid back, in an old age of honourable ease, his mother's long life of anxiety for him. He might have given to her out of his strength what she out of her weakness had given to him. He might have won from the world its acknowledgment of merit in the shape of titles and degrees, and yet all the while the heart of him, the true manhood within him, have been hard and dead. Pride and duty can never bring a man's life up to its highest level. They may make it very noble and very worthy, but they can never put upon it the crown of fair completeness. Only a woman's hand puts that crown on.

And here the chivalry which does not always, or only spring of lofty lineage, or need the surroundings of gentle birth to nourish its fair flower, did for Stephen Garton what an early, fast-rooted love does for some men. For his ideal, as they do for their real, he lived a sweet, pure life. Lowly-born, uncultivated man though he was, wanting sometimes in the outward shows of politeness, honest rather than graceful in his speech and bearing, there yet lay hidden far down in the heart of him, like flowers under the brown leaves of autumn, the jewel of true knightliness and courtesy, the which, cherishing intact, any man, however simple his descent, however lowly his surroundings, is one of Nature's true nobility.

Stephen took no praise to himself for this. He did not so much as know that to keep his heart fresh and pure for the woman

whose love he some day hoped to win, was
anything for which a man needed praise.
He felt his face grow hot sometimes, when
his gay young fellow-students spoke lightly
of some fair girl to whom they were, as they
called it, "making up;" perhaps displaying a
scrap of her writing, or a riband she had
worn, as a trophy of their conquest. And
he could have laid them sprawling on the
ground with one blow of his strong fist, as
they counted over the maidens whose smiles
they had won, and whose faces had flushed
for flattering words of theirs. They did not
seem to think there was any harm in it, but
Stephen Garton felt that rather than have
spoken such words, or talked in such a tone
of any woman who had ever looked gently
upon him, he would have struck off his right
hand.

Perhaps he was foolish in having such

exalted ideas of womanly honour. Perhaps
when he mixed more freely with the great
world of society, and became accustomed to
pretty faces, and bright eyes, and bewitch-
ing smiles, and found, to his cost, that these
did not always go along with perfect truthfulness and unsullied purity of heart, he
would learn to take down a few of his lofty
notions, and mitigate his indignation for a
light word or two, spoken against those who
were, after all, as capable of fighting their
own battles with the small fire of coquetry
and flirtation, as he was capable of defending
them with his heavy artillery of honour and
knightliness.

But that was how he felt, when, in those
young student days, he waited for his Hermione to descend from her pedestal and
walk hand-in-hand with him through life.

CHAPTER II.

ANOTHER competitor for the Burton scholarship was Rodney Charnock, the fashionable young gentleman for whose welfare Stephen had not long ago so grievously imperilled his own. Rodney had an average share of ability when he chose to exert it, but he lacked the steady, plodding perseverance which kept Stephen Garton's talents always marshalled on the field, and apart from which the most brilliant gifts are often like troops without a general, able to parade effectively at a review, but useless in time of action. Now, however, Rodney was working more industriously than usual, for the College term closed in June, and when the next commenced in September the scholarship was to be awarded.

There was a tacit feud between Charnock and Stephen Garton, which all Stephen's little acts of generosity and forbearance could not put away. Nor, indeed, were such acts intended to put it away, for Stephen did really and heartily dislike his fellow-student. He could have fought and floored him with the supremest satisfaction; and nothing but a spirit of honourable benevolence, which he was rather ashamed than otherwise of possessing, kept him from wiping out Charnock's innumerable acts of petty insult in some such summary fashion.

For the young man, who prided himself upon belonging to one of the best families in the neighbourhood, was perpetually twitting Stephen with his lowly origin, and passing what he considered facetious remarks on the smallness of his wardrobe, and the scanty adornments of his sanctum upstairs. Once he had gone so far as to say something about the "old woman at Millsmany," but an ominous glitter in Stephen's eye warned him that it would be dangerous to proceed. And Rodney, like most other small people, had a noticeable vein of prudence in his composition. He preferred giving a succession of little stabs, none of them actually recognizable by law, to one straightforward, downright thrust, which might lay him open to unpleasant consequences. And his adversary's very forbearance over these little stabs, as, indeed, Stephen might have known, had his acquaintance with the world been wider, only increased the spite with which Rodney gave them; just as the leisurely patience of a great St. Bernard dog only irritates still more the little cur which is yelping and snapping at its heels.

Rodney could not forget that circumstance about the upsetting of the Governor's bookcase. He had never been able to look Stephen right in the face since. He always wanted to skulk past him when they met each other alone. Stephen's quiet unconscious bearing seemed like a perpetual rebuke to his own meanness, for he had conscience enough to know that he *had* been mean. His dislike of the " charity student," as he called him, which, when Stephen first came to the college, had been more a whim than anything else, was now fast deepening into real enmity. There would be a smash some day, the other young men said, between these two—a regular encounter and clearing up, and then perhaps they would shake hands over their differences and be friends.

The students were wrong there, though. Stephen Garton and Rodney Charnock never would be friends, come what might.

Stephen had never made any explanation to the Governor about his conduct in the common hall, and Dr. Ellesley was too proud to ask it. The barrier which springs up so quickly between two sensitive natures, and which, once acknowledged, is so hard to forget, parted between them now. The one word which might have thrown it down, Stephen could not bring himself to speak. But the cold courtesy of the Doctor's manner since that night's disturbance chafed and irritated him. He began to feel bitter and sarcastic, as people are apt to feel when they find themselves thrust into a wrong position. He was learning to set himself in an attitude of defiance against the world in general, to accuse friendship of being hollow, and kindliness a

cheat, and to cultivate in private that sublime
scorn which answers admirably for an epic
poem, but makes such a very poor figure
in everyday life. He had no one to help
him, no one to set him straight, and show
him that he was only going through what
most men of strong and tender feelings must
go through before they come to anything like
ripeness of experience. If he had had a woman friend to speak a kind word to him now
and then, a sister who believed in him as
sisters do sometimes believe in their brothers,
and who could have turned the sunlight of
her loving heart upon him when his own was
passing through the cloud, then he might
have laughed away his bitterness, or put it
aside as a thing neither wise nor expedient.
But he had no sister, no woman friend in
all the world, except his mother; and she,
kind, good, loving as she was, lived a life

quite apart from his. She looked up to him with wonder and reverence, as to one whose stores of book-knowledge set him far away from her; she could not suffer in his suffering, nor rejoice in his joy, nor give out of her scant life what he was beginning to need for his. Steve must bear his burden alone, or carry it where only the weary ever find rest.

The students were gathered in the common hall one sunny afternoon in early May. Those of them who were working for the Burton prize, except Stephen, were clustered in a little group round one of the windows, talking over their respective chances of success; for with the good-fellowship of hostile armies before the ring of battle begins, they chatted frankly enough over prospective difficulties, and compared progress in the terrible array of subjects which they were required to master before the prize examination.

Stephen, sitting alone at the other end of the room, could hear their conversation, though he took no part in it. Rodney Charnock was, as usual, one of the chief speakers. He was telling the rest of a "blocker," as he called it, to which he had come in the astronomical department of his preparations. It was a very tough problem, involving a considerable amount of mathematical skill. As likely as not it might never be touched upon by the examining professors after he had spent so much labour in the solution of it; but still if he shirked it, there was just the chance that it might cost him the prize. The other four students had not come to it yet, most of them having put off their astronomical questions to the last, and so they could give him no help.

"It's a confounded bore," said Rodney,

stroking a tiny moustache, which, after great expenditure of patience and analeptic cream, he had at last coaxed into existence upon his upper lip.

"You're quite right, Rodd," answered another of the students, Fensley by name, broad-built, heavy-looking, but with a splendid brain development. "I'm almost ready, for my part, to back out of it. It takes up an awful lot of time. I'm not half sure that a trip to Germany for three years is worth all the fag. What do you say about it, Banks?"

Banks was a fair-haired young man, one of the lay students, pale, slender, with not much stamina about him. His thin cheeks and the dark shadows under his eyes, told that this Burton prize would be a dear bargain to him, even if he won it.

"I don't know," he said languidly. "It's

more of a fag than I looked for. If you
and Charnock mean to give in, I'll join
you. I've heaps to do yet, and it's beginning to make awful hash of me, sitting up
at nights, and all that sort of thing. Suppose we do give it up—back out of the whole
concern."

"What, and let *him* have a better chance?"
said Rodney Charnock, glancing towards Stephen, and speaking in a low tone. "No, indeed, I'm not quite such a fool as all that
comes to. I don't care a screw for money
and a free trip to Germany amongst all
those mouldy professors and puffy fräuleins,
but I'll go in for it up to the very last,
just to keep him out. Fancy, Banks, what
a glorious figure the College would cut if
it got out amongst the public that a washerwoman's son had carried off the Burton
prize! Humble parentage, risen by honest

merit, struggled with early disadvantages, or something in that line, as they'll put in the papers, of course, when the winner is announced; but people know what that means well enough. I should hate to belong to the concern after that."

" Bravo, Rodney! there's a brick, boys," said Marten, the other student. "Nothing like standing up for the honour of Alma Mater, such as she is. But, after all, Rodney, he isn't quite so bad as that, is he? I had an idea he was of a decent stock, come down in the world; born of poor but pious parents, who had seen better days,—that style of thing, you know."

Rodney stroked his moustache again, and gave the ends a curl.

"A true bill, Marten. Mother takes in washing. Excellent old soul; says her prayers whilst she's starching the collars, and speaks her experience whilst she's hanging them out to dry. Blessed season of late. Much drawn out in prayer: spiritle feelins riz wonderful; feel like going to glory, right away."

And the facetious Mr. Rodney imitated the provincial accent and nasal intonation of some of the humble Christians of Millsmany.

"Hush! Rodney," said Banks, "or he'll hear you, and then we shall have a row."

"I don't care if we have," said Rodney. "I mean to get that fellow out of the College before I'm through my course. It's a positive disgrace to the place that a washerwoman's son should come and study in it."

"Especially if he carries off the Burton prize," said the lay student, meditatively.

"And from such a choice sprig of the aristocracy as you," said Fensley, looking with an air of lazy, good-natured indifference at his exquisitely-got-up fellow-student. "But I am sorry I can't help you, old boy. I haven't begun to look at my astronomy yet. They say it's the toughest part of the business, and so I'm leaving it to the last; getting myself in training for it, you know. But I say, Rodd, just think about it, and if you *do* decide to throw up, Marten and I won't stand against you."

"Trust *me,*" said Charnock. And then, putting his arm into that of the lay-student, both the young men sauntered into the College grounds.

Stephen heard what was said about the astronomical problem, but not what was said about his mother and himself. He had worked the problem only a day or two before, and knew the exact place where Charnock had stuck fast in some mathematical calculations which required more brain than he could bring to bear upon them. He had it in his heart to help his fellow-student out of the difficulty; but he did not like, by doing so publicly and openly, to put himself on a higher moral ground than Charnock was taking against him; so exalting himself, as it were, at the expense of Charnock's humiliation. That would savour too much of the Jack Horner spirit.

"See what a great boy am I!"

Stephen had read about heaping coals of fire on the head of an enemy, but he knew it was not to be done by going up to that enemy and doing him a public kindness, with supremely virtuous complacency; saying to him, in fact—"Now, you have been behaving very badly to me, but I have come to let you see how generous and forgiving I can be to you; and though you deserve that I should do you a bad turn, yet I am going to do you a good one instead, and I hope you feel properly obliged to me for it." Stephen despised that sort of thing. He was quite sure he should never feel anything like a sensation of burning, if the coals were heaped upon *him* in such a style as that. He would ten times rather have the cool, measured courtesy with which Dr. Ellesley, fancying him an enemy, was treating him now, than that abominably bland complacency which characterizes some men's forgiveness. All the pride, and all the reserve, and all the loftiness of his nature rebelled against it. He could not go and say to his fellow-student—

"Charnock, I'll work that problem for you if you like. I've done it before."

He could not say it before the rest of the students, because that would humiliate Charnock and exalt himself. He could not go and say it to him privately, because that would seem to imply that he wanted to shake hands and be friends. And he did *not* want to do that. He would ten times rather keep as he was, cool, distant, unconscious. He judged Charnock by himself. And he knew that if *he* had behaved badly to anyone, and that one, instead of quietly keeping away from him, had thrust himself into his presence, and assumed friendly relations with him, he should have been ready to strike him down there and then for daring to over-step that boundary line of respect which is sacred between enemy and enemy, as much as between friend and friend.

At last he thought of a plan by which he might put the desired information in Charnock's way, without the young man himself, or anyone else, knowing about it. He could refer to the chapter in one of the examination-books, a chapter apparently overlooked by Charnock, giving the key to the working of the problem which had blocked him. If that chapter could be placed before him, he would get from it just what he wanted, and then go triumphantly on.

Stephen watched the two students, Rodney and Banks, sauntering down the beech-tree avenue which led into the fields. They were nearly half-way down. Even if they turned directly and came back, he should have time to do what he wanted before they reached the College again.

He put the little book he had been reading into his pocket, and went into Charnock's study only a door or two beyond his own. Exercise papers were lying about, scraps of calculations, reference books; amongst them that which contained the needful information. Stephen picked it out, found the chapter, the page, the paragraph, and laid the book upon the table, with another on the top of it to keep the leaves from blowing over. Then he put a pencil mark against the paragraph, such as Charnock himself used for any places to which he might need to refer. He was careless and unmethodical in his studies. He would never notice that the book had been moved, or that the pencil-mark was not his own. And when he came up in the evening, and set to work again upon the problem which was still spread out upon the table, he would just take up the book, thinking he had put it there himself; and then, as if by accident, find what he wanted.

That little act of kindness, unseen, unacknowledged, unrecorded, save in a book which human eyes never look upon, might cost Stephen Garton the coveted scholarship. It might give his opponent an advantage over him, which could never be won back again. But cost what it might, he could not help doing it. Nay, that it needed to be done for a man whom he counted as his enemy, only made it the more binding upon him; and that it was done without thought or prospect of reward, did not make it seem more noble to the simple-hearted man from whom it came.

CHAPTER III.

AFTER that Stephen went out into the College grounds, purposely avoiding the beech-tree avenue, lest he might meet Rodney Charnock there.

He did not feel on such admirable terms with himself as most men would have felt, after such a deed of unselfish generosity. Stephen's conscience did not often reward him with a sugar-plum of approval, and he did not think, in this case, that he particularly deserved it. For, after all, he had not felt kindly towards Rodney Charnock. He did not even want to feel kindly towards him. It did not give him any great trouble or uneasiness to know that all was not quite straight between them.

"If thine enemy hunger, feed him," that was hard enough, especially when the feeding of the enemy might lead to the starving of the man who had fed him. But to love that enemy too. Ah! that was more than Stephen Garton could accomplish. And he did not even greatly desire to have such a spirit as would enable him to do it.

Still the performing of that act of kindness had done him good. Like all noble thoughts, cherished and acted out, it had brought into his soul the element of rest, and made him more at peace with himself. Nay, there was even springing up within him a little germ of good-will towards this young man who had wronged him so often. Just then, it was hard for him to cherish bitter thoughts towards anyone. He would rather have been at one with all the world, if it would have let him, if it would only not misunderstand and vex him so. Stephen was not thoroughly at rest yet, far from it; but he felt then what he had not felt for a long time, that he would be willing to shake hands with any man in the world, Rodney Charnock included, if that man wished it.

In this frame of mind he strolled across the lawn towards the shrubbery which led to a farm belonging to the College, and thence to the Carriden-Regis woods. The afternoon was very still and quiet. Long shadows lay upon the grass, with belts of sunshine between them; slant sunshine, which quivering upward, turned to coral the transparent stems of the young sycamores, and shot many a golden arrow through and through the white-blossomed hawthorns.

It was a time for peacefulness and content, and Stephen opened his heart to both. Rough and uncouth as some people thought **him**, he was very sensitive to surrounding influences. It made all the difference in the world to him, whether a clear blue sky bent over him as now, or grey murky clouds shut the sunshine from that little den of his, which had so much need of all the brightness it could get; whether the warm breath of the south stirred the ivy leaves outside his window, or the biting east winds brought him their store of smoke and blacks from the great town of Millsmany. And a primrose or a violet, peering out through hedgeside moss to tell him spring had come, did more to freshen him up and make him study with right good will, than a whole flask of Cognac or a bundle of the best cigars that Havannah ever produced could have done; did it more cheaply, too, which was a consideration with Stephen Garton.

Close by the gate of the College grounds he met Banks and Charnock. He did not see them until they were close upon him, and then it was too late to turn aside. Banks gave him a friendly nod; he was a good-hearted fellow, and generally managed to keep straight with the rest of the students; but Charnock plucked the sleeve of his somewhat seedy coat as he passed, and said with jocose familiarity—

"Clothes come home from the wash, Dame Garton, eh? Mind you get them a good colour this time."

Stephen made no answer. He stood for a moment or two like one stunned. This sudden sweeping away of all the little buds of kindness and good-will which had been springing up within him, was almost too

much. His first impulse was to go and hold
Charnock by the throat until he had choked
him, or to fell him to the ground and stamp
the life out of him. He felt like some wild
animal hunted down and goaded to the last
degree of endurance. Then in a tumult of
mingled passion and sorrow, Rodney's mock-
ing laugh ringing in his ears, Rodney's
touch thrilling through him, he hurried on
through the meadows and across the corn-
fields, anywhere—anywhere, so that that man's
face might not come up before him again,
so that he might forget those cruel words,
or think within himself now for the first time
how to repay them with crueller.

No more warmth of May sunshine for him,
no more sweetness of hawthorn and lilac
from the blossoming hedgerows. The daisies
might look up into his face, asking smile
for smile, but he had none to give them;

the delicate woodruff might tell its fragrant
story as he crushed it beneath his feet—he
never staid to listen. On he went, not caring where nor how, until the path grew
tangled and the briers tore his hands, and
great thickets of wild roses, and copses
where the hazel grew, told him that he had
come to the Carriden-Regis wood, a mile
away from home.

It was of little consequence to him where
he was, only that rough tangled path gave
him something to fight against and overcome.
There was a sort of satisfaction in treading
down the young hazel twigs and stamping
their tender buds into the earth, and striking away the tall green brackens which
stretched out their hands to him from the
shady covert of the wood. If he could
have pushed away all good and gentle
thoughts so; if he could have crushed up

all his kindness and tenderness just as he was crushing up these harmless little green leaves, how well it would have been. What was a man's heart good for, but to mock him? What was benevolence but a great sham, and honour but a cheat, and goodness but a delusion? And what had all these years of honest striving and endeavour done for him, but educate him into a state in which he could feel more keenly the whips and stings of monied ignorance? Better if he had never tried to get out of the old narrow groove where nature and circumstance first placed him. Better if he had gone and toiled in some Millsmany factory, sat behind a loom all his life, or spent his time in greasing cranks and pulleys, knowing nothing of the soul within him, or even that he had a soul at all. It had been better far—more to his comfort in every way.

Thinking such thoughts as these, Stephen crushed his way through the briers and thorns, feeling splendidly heroic, so far as his mental state was concerned, but physically very uncomfortable, by reason of the scratches he had received during his progress. However, he had worse scratches than these to think about now. He tore along, not caring where he went, only feeling that he must keep pushing on somewhere, away from the college and Rodney Charnock, until he came to an open space in the wood where two or three paths met, one of them the nearest foot-road to Carriden-Regis.

Here, spent, not so much with bodily fatigue as with the tumult of passionate excitement which Charnock's taunts had produced, he threw himself down on the grass, letting the wind play through his hair, and the little fern leaves lay their cool touch upon his face. Sunshine enough pierced the trees to make here and there a golden streak through the long glades of the wood, and like a soft grey shadow under the trees the great beds of wild hyacinth bloomed, sending their sweet perfume to him upon every breath of wind. For sound, too, the blackbirds were piping merrily enough in the thorn-bushes, and the thrushes answering with sweet saucy song; and when these were still, the wood-pigeon told her plaintive tale from the larch-trees' topmost branch.

But Stephen had no heart to listen. He was only thinking how he might best get away from the college, and plunge into downright hard work somewhere—work that would keep his old mother from need of toil, and himself from such taunts as empty-head-ed striplings heaped upon him for thrusting himself out of his proper place. He did not care how mean the work was; perhaps the meaner the better, for then no one could cast up against him his lowly birth, or tell him that he was holding too high the head which Providence had meant to stoop over a day labourer's drudgery. Already in the heat of his angry impatience he had gathered up his books and closed his study door for the last time, and bidden farewell to the Governor, and set out to be a hero in the strife elsewhere, out of reach of the gibes of fashionable young aristocrats or brainless lay students. Already he saw himself, in check shirt and canvas cap, oiling machinery in one of those immense factories, the smoke of whose chimneys he could see, seven miles away, through one of the glades in the wood; or helping to load or unload the huge trucks of raw and manufactured produce which were for ever coming and going past the mills and warehouses. And then good-bye to his fine dreams of future name and fame, of a comfortable old age for his mother, and a love-lighted home for himself. For he should never find his Hermione among the mill-girls of that great, busy, bustling town, and from no more lofty pedestal than they occupied would she step down to put her hand in his. He must be content to go through the world without her.

As Stephen Garton lay upon the grass thinking these altogether grand and heroic thoughts, he heard footsteps in the distance, footsteps upon the dry, withered, last-year's leaves, which had drifted into the pathway amongst the tender little spring buds. Some one was coming that way. Surely not Rodney Charnock, though?—the saints preserve him from the presence of that dainty lay student for a few hours longer, at any rate!

Stephen rolled himself over and over a few times, until through some tall bracken stems he could look down the glade from which the sounds came. No, thank goodness! it was not Rodney Charnock. It was a woman dressed in black; a long way down the glade too, though in the stillness of that May afternoon her footfall could be distinctly heard. He watched her as she came nearer and nearer, and soon discovered that she was not in the ordinary acceptation of the word a "woman," meaning thereby a person of humble, low-bred aspect and manner; but a lady, and a young lady too, with a certain easy girlish grace in every step and motion. She had a bunch of lilies of the valley in her hand—they grew nowhere so richly as in Carriden-Regis wood—and she often stopped to gather more from the moss where they clustered in great beds round the beech-tree trunks. Such a pretty little figure, all in black, not a touch of colour anywhere about her, but the lily leaves in her hands, and a sheen as of gold where the sunlight caught her hair, and a rosy flush upon her face, which, as she came nearer and nearer to him, Stephen thought was fair enough for the Hermione of his dreams.

He scrambled to his feet, and began to consider what he should do. He would have struck off into one of the copses, out of sight, only the young lady was so close upon him now, that his doing so would have frightened her. If he skulked out of the way anywhere, she might think he was a vagabond or a poacher, and so be afraid to go past. And, indeed, when he began to take a survey of his personal appearance, he was compelled to admit that a suspicion

of that sort was not altogether unwarrant-
able. Such a tug as he had had through
the briers and brambles, though admirably
adapted to foster his heroic notions of dis-
comfort and self-mortification, had not by
any means tended to the beautifying of the
outer man. A lady, especially a young and
pretty lady, as this one appeared to be,
might well be excused for hurrying past
him with a little flutter of something like
fear, seeing that there was no one within
call if he attempted rudeness or insult.

At last Stephen determined that the wisest
thing he could do would be to sit down
on one of the fallen trunks, and appear to be studying the little book which
he had put into his pocket an hour ago,
when he went into Rodney Charnock's room
to do him that very needless piece of kindness about the astronomical problem. Ac-

cordingly, he smoothed his hair, and put on his cap, and shook the dry leaves and bits of moss from his coat, and opening his book at the twelfth proposition of Euclid, tried to look at any rate so harmless and peaceable, that a lady, passing alone and unattended, need not be afraid of him.

Evidently this lady was not. For after looking at him some time as she came along, he meanwhile studying his proposition very diligently, she stepped aside out of the path to him, and said—

"Can you tell me if one of these paths leads into the meadows belonging to the College farm?"

With instinctive courtesy Stephen sprang to his feet, and raised his cap, now for the first time looking into her face as she addressed him. He thought it was a pleasant face, the pleasantest and fairest he had ever seen; and although by her bearing and accent he could tell that she was a gentlewoman born, there was not the slightest air of condescension or patronage in her way of putting the question; still less of that freezing coldness with which English people generally speak to strangers.

"Yes," he said, "there is a road out to the meadows; this one before you. You must follow it about a hundred yards, and then take a little footpath to your right, you will know it by an old willow stump, and a bed of lilies like those you have in your hand. And then that will lead you——"

"Oh! stay," said the lady, laughing. "I am sure I shall never be able to remember all that. I shall be lost again directly. Is there not some nearer way into the Millsmany high-road?"

"Not that I know of," said Stephen. "But I am sure you cannot miss your way. The first turning to your right, and then the first to your left, and that will lead you to the gate which opens into the meadows. And when you once get into the meadows, you have nothing to do but keep along the flagged path until you come past the College into the high-road."

"Thank you," said the young lady, turning away. "I am very much obliged to you."

And then she went back into the path, not very certain, Stephen thought, from a slight hesitation in her manner, whether she should be able to find the right way, after all.

"Stay," he said, stuffing the twelfth proposition into his pocket. "If you will let me, I will go with you and show you the road as far as the meadow. I am one of the students at the College, and I know it well enough."

Again that clear, honest, questioning glance, with which she spoke to him at first; again the same apparent confidence in what it read, for without any further hesitation or embarrassment, she thanked him, and they both set off together.

Stephen Garton was not quite unaccustomed to what is called "society." His private teaching in Millsmany and the neighbourhood of Carriden-Regis had taken him amongst people who considered themselves his superiors, and who did not scruple to let him know that fact by a certain elaborate condescension in their manners, or—which was almost more galling than the condescension—a patronizing familiarity, quickly changing into icy neglect, if, during the course of the lesson, or the half hour which his employers sometimes invited him to stay beyond it, visitors were announced. If, when the ladies of the family were alone, he **was** allowed the privilege of a little conversation with them, he was always given to understand that on no account must that privilege be assumed, save when they chose to grant it. And to do Stephen justice, he rarely presumed upon such kindness as the good people of Millsmany and Carriden-Regis accorded to him. Perhaps he had discernment enough to take it for what it was worth, and to wait for his position in society until he could claim it without any need of patronage.

But this girl's manner towards him was so very different. Whoever she might be, whatever her rank in life—and Stephen felt that she belonged to a higher class than the wealthy Millsmany upstarts—she met him

now with the frank cordiality of an equal.
Nay, there was something more than cordiality in her manner, there was the courtesy
of one who is receiving a kindness. Evidently she did not think, as some young and
graceful ladies in similar circumstances would
have thought, that she was doing the student a favour by allowing him to show her
what she could not find out for herself;
neither did she entrench herself behind the
barrier of a prudent silence, and intimate
to him in that way that although she was
compelled to accept his companionship for
a short distance, still he was by no means
to consider himself on that account at
liberty to enter into conversation, or in any
way conduct himself as other than an animated finger-post, a convenience to be
dropped as soon as circumstances would
permit of the dropping. On the contrary,

she began at once to talk to him in an easy unaffected way about the country, and the scenery, and to listen with eager interest as he told her about the pleasant walks, Stephen knew them every one, which were within reach of the village, either down the beautiful Carriden valley, or across those great brown moors, so rich in fern and heather and wild flowers, which lay eastward towards Millsmany. He even found himself by-and-by—he so lately waging warfare in his thoughts with all the world, determined to shut himself up within his own individuality, and never make a friend of man nor woman again—talking to this stranger lady about his College and the Burton prize for which he was competing—she had heard of that prize, and so she could not be quite a stranger, he thought—and telling her what subjects they had to get up for it.

To all of which she listened with a frank,
unaffected interest, which made Stephen think
that perhaps he had been mistaken after all
in thinking that the world was such a very
great cheat, and that nobody in it, except
his mother and the Governor of Carriden-
Regis College, was worth caring for.

Soon, much too soon for Stephen, who
could have wished that woodland path many
times as long, they reached the gate which
opened into the meadows.

"I must leave you here, I suppose," he
said. "You will find the road quite easily
now. Go straight through the fields, one
after another, until you come to the College, and then you are close upon the
high-road."

"Thank you again," said the lady. "It is
very kind of you to have taken so much
trouble for me."

And then she added, looking brightly up into his face, and it was far to look, too, for Stephen was tall of stature, and Meta Waldemar was but a little creature—

"If you belong to the College, I shall very likely see you again, sometimes; for I know Mrs. Ellesley, and she has asked me to come and see her as often as I like. Good-bye."

Then she left him. He stood there, watching her as she tripped along so lightly over the footpath, now and then turning off into the grass to add a violet or a primrose to the posy in her hand. She was such a bright, winsome, trustful little thing. She had taken so readily and unsuspiciously, what he offered to give her, taken it, too, as friend might take from friend, and not stranger from stranger. Stephen had shut the gate between him and all lovely, pleasant things before this young girl came to him in the Carriden-Regis wood; now he opened it again, feeling that having only the memory, if nothing else, of her smile and look, and voice, it could quite close upon him no more.

Not until she was out of sight did he turn away, and with a strange new brightness flooding all his thoughts, go back to the beech-tree clearing, there to dream away the hours until the slant sunshine, striking up through the tall brackens, beyond which he had first caught sight of Meta Waldemar, should bid him back again to the College and to study.

And with what new vigour could he study now; with what new calmness and resolve. How completely had that girl's face swept away all the angry, bitter thoughts which had been surging to and fro within him! As mists when the sun rises, they had all dispersed. A new life lay before him. His Hermione, so long dreamed of but unreal hitherto, had descended from her pedestal, and stood before him in all the warm, sweet grace of womanhood. Whether she would clasp hands with him and be his companion for the rest of the way, he knew not; but this he knew, unless she did it, that way would be henceforth always lonely.

CHAPTER IV.

THIS was how it happened that Meta Waldemar and Stephen Garton met in the Carriden-Regis wood on that pleasant May afternoon.

Mrs. Waldemar had only been waiting for the Doctor's possible call of ceremony, to make a visit with Meta to Mrs. Ellesley. Meta had delivered the old lady's message.

"Tell your mother, with my kind regards, that I hope she will bring you to see me very soon."

Mrs. Waldemar thought she knew what that meant. It meant that Mrs. Ellesley, as

well as her son, was willing, and even anxious to be friendly, and had thus taken advantage of Meta's home-coming to secure
more frequent intercourse between the two
families. Because, of course, it was simply
impossible that either the Doctor or his mother should care anything about the companionship of a girl like Meta, so shy and retiring, with absolutely nothing in the world to
say for herself, not a bit of conversational
ability or sprightliness about her; the very
idea of such a thing was absurd in the extreme. But that they should desire the companionship of a person like herself—a person
accustomed to society, cultivated, fascinating,
capable of making herself so very agreeable,
as the late Mr. Waldemar used to tell her
fifty times a day, poor dear man! she could
make herself when she tried—that was an
idea not at all absurd, quite the contrary.

Indeed, Mrs. Waldemar thought it was the most natural thing in the world that Dr. Ellesley, who, of course, had been the originator of that message about calling, should be anxious to follow up his introduction at Percy Cottage. But being so painfully shy, as the nervous hesitation of his manners proclaimed him to be, and perhaps, also, not being sufficiently sure of his ground to make any advances in his own proper person, he had thus sheltered himself behind his mother and Meta, paying that attention to the younger which a due regard to expediency at the present immature stage of the proceedings prevented him from offering to the older lady, though in reality intended for her.

And really, as Mrs. Waldemar said to herself, when she came to look seriously at it, that home-coming of Meta's, which at first sight had appeared such an unmitigated nuisance, might turn out to be rather favourable to her own prospects than otherwise. For, under pretext of taking Meta into society, and giving her a proper introduction to the world, which at her age was the very thing she required, many visits might be paid, and many invitations given, which, had they been paid and given on her own account, would have afforded subject for ill-natured comments from the village gossips, Mrs. Danesborough in particular, who was always so very ready to pick up anything to the disadvantage of her neighbours. Really it was astonishing how things always did present a smooth handle to people who were sensible enough to take hold of it.

So thought Mrs. Waldemar, as she arrayed herself with becoming care before setting off with Meta to call upon Mrs. Ellesley, a few days after the Doctor's visit to Percy Cottage, Miss Hacklebury being left at home to keep house.

Dorothy Ann rarely went out to make calls, except upon the old people in her district who needed herb tonics; neither did her sister press that duty upon her as she pressed the duties of rent-paying, dividend-collecting, superintendence of repairs, ordering in of stores, and other more laborious departments of the domestic economy. For to tell the truth, sister Dorothy Ann was not at all effective in a morning call. Neither her style of dress, accent, manners, nor general deportment were calculated to produce an impression favourable to the social position of the family. She was so very ordinary, or perhaps Mrs. Waldemar might say, considering her extreme bluntness and straightforwardness, extraordinary, in the presence of strangers. And then, too, Mrs. Waldemar never felt quite herself in Dorothy Ann's company. She could not launch out to the full extent of her fascinations when fettered by the consciousness of a third party, and that a party, too, who knew her so well, She did not exactly like to talk about being " so impulsive, you know," so delicately sensitive to affection, so passionately fond of having some one to pet and caress, when all the while sister Dorothy Ann was sitting opposite, bolt upright, her shawl squared over her shoulders, her bonnet-strings sticking out so fiercely, her hands firmly gripped together —Dorothy Ann had no idea of disposing of her hands gracefully during a morning call —with a grave, incredulous look upon her face, knowing that she never got so much as a kiss out of sister Waldemar for months together. Though, of course, as Mrs. Waldemar used to say, people were not expected to be so sweetly impulsive in the bosom of their families; it was more a thing for outward manifestation, like one's best dresses and most expensive jewelry, too good for every-day wear.

And then Dorothy Ann was so very incautious in talking about their past circumstances; never seemed to have any idea of keeping back the fact that when they lived in Poplarcroft, after Mr. Hacklebury had retired from business, they only kept a small girl to do the rough work, and helped in the cooking themselves. Nay, so far from keeping it back, she seemed to have a sort of pride in it, and would even, if the people they were calling upon gave her the slightest encouragement, dive into the very thick of household affairs; tell them the best method of making bread so as to ensure its rising, or the neatest way of getting up fine linen and doing starch things so as to keep them from sticking to the iron, just as if all her life had been devoted to that sort of thing. Whereas Mrs. Waldemar, when she was left to herself, directed the conversation in such a very different line. No one, to hear Mrs. Waldemar talk, would think that the family had been accustomed to anything less than a full staff of servants and everything carried on in the best style. So Dorothy Ann was left at home whilst Mrs. Waldemar and her step-daughter set off to the College.

But even that walk, simple a thing as it appeared, could not be done without a little previous planning on the part of the elder lady. It is a noticeable fact that when people have once given themselves up to the

art of contrivance, they lose the power of
acting straightforwardly, even when there is
no need for concealment. Their scheming
becomes a habit; they cannot do even the
simplest thing without it. Mrs. Waldemar
had her own little piece of private management about that walk. She knew that Meta
wanted to go round by the Carriden-Regis
wood, Dr. Ellesley having spoken of that
way as so much pleasanter, though nearly
a mile further than the turnpike road. Accordingly, when they reached the stile which
led into the woods, and Meta proposed that
they should cross it, she hesitated, fancied
she felt symptoms of an approaching headache, thought it would scarcely be prudent
for her to walk so far round, and finally decided to go by the turnpike herself, leaving
Meta to go through the wood alone.

"I am afraid of the damp," she said,

querulously. "I feel it strike through me as soon as ever I set foot in a place that never gets the sun. And the insects, too, and all that sort of thing, are such a nuisance. I can't bear a wood, it was always my aversion. I wonder at your taste, preferring those nasty damp paths to this beautiful clean high road; but as your poor dear papa used to say, I never was like other people. I had such refinement, could never bear to look at anything coarse like those nasty insects and creeping things one sees in woods. But don't hurry yourself, Meta, if you like to leave me. If you do reach the College a few minutes after me, it is of no consequence. And do, my dear, be careful not to get anything on your dress. I never feel myself safe for days after I have been in the neighbourhood of earwigs or spiders, or any of those awful creatures that infest shady places."

And with this pleasantly suggestive re-commendation to her step-daughter, Mrs. Waldemar pursued her way along the high road, just as she had intended to do from the very first. For she knew that by taking that road she should arrive at the College a full half hour, if not more, before Meta, who had such a fancy for stopping every half dozen yards to collect sticks and mos-ses, and bits of grass, and all that sort of nonsense. And half an hour alone with dear old Mrs. Ellesley would be very desirable under present circumstances. Moreover, if Meta lingered very long in the wood, her late arrival at the College might involve tea there, and a walk home in the evening under the Governor's protection, both of which chances, falling out by the merest accident, might be productive of advantageous results.

Mrs. Waldemar was quite successful in the first part of her little arrangement. She had had fully three quarters of an hour's chat with Mrs. Ellesley before Meta, with her hands full of grasses and wild flowers, made her appearance in the College drawing-room. The solicitor's widow was all smiles and affection. She was never anything else in the presence of strangers.

"Well, Meta, my pet, I am so glad you have come at last. Do you know, my darling, I began to be so fearfully nervous about you. I was afraid something dreadful had happened to you in the wood. Now did I not say, dear Mrs. Ellesley, that I was so terribly afraid something had happened to her in the woods? And have you enjoyed yourself very much, my sweet?"

"Yes, mamma," said Meta simply. "I wish you had gone with me. It was so very beautiful in some parts. Only if you don't care about woods, of course it makes a difference. I am so sorry you don't care about them."

Mrs. Waldemar looked sharply across to her step-daughter, to warn her from trespassing farther on that subject. For she had been saying to Mrs. Ellesley, just before Meta came in, how much she regretted not having been able to go with her pet through the Carriden-Regis wood. She did so dote upon the beauties of Nature, she said, there was scarcely anything she doted upon so passionately as the beauties of Nature. And finding in the Doctor's mother a genuine admirer of the same, she had launched out even more than usual into rapturous praises of sylvan scenery. There was nothing in the world, she affirmed, that charmed her half so much as sylvan scenery, and it was such a grief to her that her exceedingly delicate state of health did not allow her to revel in it more continually. Meta's little speech came in therefore rather awkwardly. She must have a little of her step-daughter's transparency and simplicity rubbed off, if possible. People who always spoke the truth were a terrible nuisance sometimes.

"I lost my way, though," said Meta, "and I don't know how long I should have been finding it, but I saw a man sitting reading on a tree-trunk—a gentleman, I mean ; one of the students he said he was, and I asked him the road, and he came with me as far as the meadows."

"Oh, my *darling!*" said Mrs. Waldemar, "how *could* you? What astonishing nerve you have, to be sure. Isn't it wonderful,

Mrs. Ellesley?" and she turned to that lady, whose countenance, however, did not indicate any unusual surprise. "Is it not really *wonderful?* Do you know if I had met such a thing as a man in the wood, when I was going through it, alone, I should have gone into hysterics directly. I'm sure I should. I should have taken it for granted at *once* that he was a poacher or a vagabond or something dreadful of that sort. Oh, Meta darling! how could you summon up courage to speak to him? Dear, you have given me quite a shock with the very idea of it."

And Mrs. Waldemar had recourse to her gold vinaigrette.

"Oh! but, mamma, I was not a bit afraid after he had told me he was one of the students. And then even before that I knew from his face I could trust him."

"Oh! Meta, you foolish darling. Now *is* she not a foolish little creature, Mrs. Ellesley? this Meta of mine; how *can* you tell from a stranger's face whether you can trust him or not?"

"I don't know, mamma, but I can; and you see I was not mistaken about him. He told me that he was a divinity student, and that he was trying for the Burton scholarship.

"Indeed!" said Mrs. Ellesley, "I wonder which of them it would be. Only six are trying now. Do you remember what he was like?"

"Yes. He was a good height, about as tall as Dr. Ellesley, and stooped a little like Dr. Ellesley, too. And he didn't look very tidy, and he walked as if he had never been to a dancing-school."

"Ah! then," said Mrs. Ellesley, smiling,

" I know him. It was Stephen Garton. Yes, I am sure it was Stephen Garton. He does walk just in that way, and looks dreadfully seedy, sometimes. But he is very clever. He is one of my son's most promising students. Fergus says he is quite sure Stephen Garton will be an honour to the College some day."

" Dear me! you don't say so," put in Mrs. Waldemar, beginning to think that perhaps after all Meta had not done such a very unwise thing when she addressed this stranger in the wood without the ceremony of a previous introduction. " How *very* funny to think that Meta should have happened upon one of the Governor's most promising students. And is he indeed so *very* clever, dear Mrs. Ellesley?"

" So my son says. One of the cleverest young men in the College. He has had to struggle with great disadvantages, too, in early life, and to make his position entirely by his own exertions."

"Dear me! how *very* romantic! Meta, my pet, I begin to feel quite sorry that I allowed you to go through the wood without me. I should so have enjoyed meeting this gifted stranger. You know, dear Mrs. Ellesley, I do so worship talent, especially when it has risen from the ranks. There is nothing I worship so much as talent. In fact, I have a perfect woman's weakness for it. Poor dear Mr. Waldemar used always to say I ought to have been the wife of a literary man, I should have looked up to him with such adoring reverence. Only, you see, Providence ordered my lot differently."

And Mrs. Waldemar sighed.

"But I have not lost my weakness for

intellectual powers in a man. I *do* think intellectual power in a man is fascinating, so *infinitely* beyond any mere gifts of money or position. Now, don't you think so, dear Mrs. Ellesley? *Do* say you think so, now, I do so love to have my friends agree with me in everything."

Mrs. Ellesley allowed that intellect was a very good thing in its way, if it did not lead a man to neglect, or overlook, the more practical duties of life. The worst of literary men, she thought, was, that they sometimes forgot social sympathies in their ardour for their own special pursuits. Very literary men, she said, were not always the pleasantest to live with.

"Ah! my dear Mrs. Ellesley!" exclaimed Mrs. Waldemar, clasping her hands with enthusiasm, "that is *so* like you. You are always so admirably practical and sensible in your views and opinions. Now you know I am *all* impulse. I can't be rational, I *really* can't, if I try ever so much. Oh! you don't know how I try sometimes to be sober and commonplace like other people, but it is really no use. As poor dear Mr. Waldemar used to say, I ought not to be judged by the standard of ordinary people, because you know I'm so very impulsive, and all that sort of thing; and I'm so apt to let my imagination run away with me. But I *do* dote upon talent, and I *should* like to see this stranger of yours, Meta. Only you know I must say I should have been so dreadfully frightened. I should have run away and hid myself in some out-of-the-way place, for fear he should attack me. I am so foolishly nervous. I don't believe there is another woman in the world such a bundle of nerves as I am. Isn't it foolish, dear Mrs. Ellesley, to be so nervous? But you know I cannot help it."

Mrs. Ellesley did not say anything. Only a quiet smile passed over her face, which Mrs. Waldemar took as an indication of sympathy with her own intensely suscepti-ble nervous organization. And she con-tinued,

"But Meta is so different. I do believe she does not know what fear is, or else I should never think of such a thing as al-lowing her to go into the Carriden-Regis woods alone. Temperaments differ, you know, so wonderfully, as poor dear Mr. Waldemar used to say, when he contrasted me with my sister Dorothy Ann, who is so very independent. I never saw a woman so independent as Dorothy Ann. But now, dear Mrs. Ellesley, *don't* you think it is a pity for a lady to be so very independent? Don't you think that a *little* nervousness and timidity is—well, is preferable? Do tell me, now, Mrs. Ellesley, what you think about it. I do so long to have your opinions about everything. You know I feel that I can depend upon you with such *perfect* confidence. Now, *don't* you think it is so much better for a woman to be clinging and properly timid, always leaning upon some one? You understand what I mean."

Mrs. Ellesley, thus called upon for her opinion, said that circumstances altered cases, and that there were times when a lady was called upon to assume a due amount of in dependence, especially when she was so placed that any help she needed must be given from herself. True independence, she said, was not shown by casting away the natural protection which Providence supplies

to most women, but by being able, when
that protection was withdrawn or withheld,
to supply its place by a wise self-reliance
and self-help. And she thought a woman
was never more to be respected than when
she was both able and willing to do for
herself that which she had no one else to
do for her.

Mrs. Waldemar was slightly disappointed.
She had intended her question to lead the
way to quite a different vein of remark. She
had expected Mrs. Ellesley deeply to sym-
pathize with her lonely situation, instead of
advising her—as her remarks seemed to imply—to be content with it and make the
best of it. However, it was useless pushing
the conversation any further in that direction, and so, after a few more general remarks, she rose to take her leave, the afternoon being already far advanced.

"I had no idea," she said, "that it was so late. Really the time seems to have flown. But congenial society, you know, congenial society does make *such* a difference. Oh! what a treasure life would be to me if I could spend it in the midst of congenial society. Some people can live without it, but I cannot. Society is *everything* to me. Oh! Mrs. Ellesley, if you were not so far away from me, if you were not *quite* so far away from me, dear Mrs. Ellesley."

Whereupon Mrs. Ellesley suggested, as the most sensible remedy for that unavoidable state of things, that when Mrs. Waldemar could walk as far as the College, she should make her visit there so much the longer, and she followed up this suggestion now by proposing that they should both stay and take a cup of tea with her, the Governor being away on business, at Millsmany.

It would be quite a charity, she said, if Meta and her mamma would stay for an hour or two, and Bateson should drive them home in the evening.

But Mrs. Waldemar was not disposed to extend her charity to Mrs. Ellesley under such circumstances.

"So kind of you, dear Mrs. Ellesley, so *very* kind; and I am sure it would have been such a pleasure to us both—would it not, Meta, my pet?—to have spent a long quiet evening with you. But poor sister Dorothy Ann would be *so* distressed; she would think something terrible had happened to us, for I did not tell her where we were going, and she fully expects us home before tea. And, you know, dear Mrs. Ellesley, I can't *bear* to distress anyone. I am so easily distressed myself, the slightest anxiety upsets me so, that really I am foolishly sensitive about the feelings of other people. But *another* evening, dear Mrs. Ellesley, it would be *such* a pleasure to me."

Mrs. Ellesley then suggested an arrangement which would have been very agreeable to Meta, namely, that she should stay at the College, whilst Mrs. Waldemar, being so affectionately careful of her sister's feelings, should go home to prevent them from being needlessly distressed. That arrangement, however, was set aside with as much ease and apparent reasonableness as its predecessor had been. Mrs. Waldemar might say what she liked about her simplicity and feminine weakness, there was not a cleverer woman in Carriden-Regis than herself at edging out of an undesirable position. And that Meta should be left in the society of Mrs. Ellesley, whilst she herself tramped home again to that of sister Dorothy Ann, was a most undesirable position, so undesirable that the very thought of it was not to be entertained for a moment.

" Oh ! *thank* you, Mrs. Ellesley ; that would be charming. I am so anxious for dear Meta to have a little congenial society; but do you know she is so painfully shy, that I cannot get her to stir into company without me ? I do believe it would be the greatest cross in the *world* to her to go out for an evening alone. Were you not saying to me the other day, Meta, my pet, that you couldn't *bear* to go into company without me ?"

Meta could not recollect having said anything of the sort. But that frequently recurring expression on her mamma's face, which she was now beginning to understand, warned her to be careful. It seemed to say—

"I know what I am about. Don't presume to contradict me."

Besides she thought that she might possibly have said something about not caring to go out at all, which, so far as she knew the Carriden-Regis people, was certainly the truth. So she held her peace, and Mrs. Waldemar continued—

"Yes, dear Mrs. Ellesley, so painfully shy, really quite a drawback to her comfort, as I very often tell her. Of course you know I feel bound to humour her just at first, the naughty little thing, because I feel it would be such a real distress for me to send her away from me; but I *must* teach her by-and-by to be a little more independent, must I not, my pet?"

And Mrs. Waldemar caressed Meta's cheek with that almost girlish playfulness which seemed to sit so naturally upon her. Every one said how beautifully Meta's step-mamma behaved to her; really it was quite charming to see the affectionateness of her manner towards the young girl, when many women in a similar position would have looked upon her coming home as quite an infliction.

These two arrangements having been plausibly set on one side, Mrs. Ellesley, as Mrs. Waldemar knew very well she would, proposed the only remaining one which was possible under the circumstances, namely, that Meta and her mamma should come to the College together at the earliest opportunity; and before that afternoon call was over, Monday, being the Governor's spare evening, had been fixed for the visit.

So far all had gone on admirably. Mrs. Waldemar could not have wished things to have fallen out better than they had done.

Only as she and her daughter walked home by the turnpike road, she took the opportunity of instilling a little wholesome counsel into Meta's mind; the gist of which counsel was, that although truthfulness, looked at in the abstract, might be an excellent thing, a very excellent thing, still there were occasions when expediency required that it should be kept judiciously in the background. And that what Meta had to learn now, was a due regard to those occasions, and a wise tact in regulating her behaviour accordingly.

CHAPTER V.

MRS. ELLESLEY, knowing that there was a Miss Hacklebury in the Percy Cottage establishment, had kindly extended her invitation to that excellent lady; but Mrs. Waldemar was far too considerate of her sister's rheumatic tendencies to hold out the faintest hope that it would be accepted.

"You know, dear Mrs. Ellesley," she said, when the Governor's mother had proposed that Miss Hacklebury should accompany them, "poor Dorothy Ann suffers so dreadfully from exposure to the weather whenever there is the slightest tendency to east wind.

You can't think how very careful I am not to allow her to run the risk of taking cold. I am sure the walk home would be quite too much for her, would it not, Meta, dear? And she was only complaining yesterday of that terrible pain, striking down into her right arm again. It is such a very distressing thing, is rheumatism. And so, dear Mrs. Ellesley, Meta and I will just come by ourselves. Dorothy Ann will not mind being left alone for one evening. Indeed, she is so charmingly unselfish, she never will let me stay in the house on her account, if she can prevent it. And, you know, at her age she begins to feel visiting a trouble. Advancing years do bring their little infirmities, do they not, dear Mrs. Ellesley?" said Mrs. Waldemar, with a gentle smile.

Mrs. Ellesley replied that they certainly *did*

bring advancing infirmities; and then she inquired what means Miss Hacklebury adopted for the relief of her rheumatism; and in the overflowing benevolence of her heart —for the Doctor's mother was one of the kindest of women—trotted away to the writing-table, and took from thence various recipes for liniments, embrocations, decoctions, and fomentations, which had been recommended to her by sundry members of the faculty for the relief of that particular ill to which human flesh, or rather human bone, is heir.

Mrs. Waldemar listened with the profoundest attention, whilst Mrs. Ellesley read over prescription after prescription, making notes of each on her ivory tablets, and professing such enthusiastic gratitude for even the remotest possibility of being able to alleviate poor dear sister Dorothy Ann's aches and pains. She would send them all, she said, that very evening, to her own druggist in Millsmany, and have them made up, and let dear Mrs. Ellesley know how they answered. She was quite sure she would never be able to get out of dear Mrs. Ellesley's debt, if any or all of them did prove efficacious. It really quite undermined the happiness of her own life to know that Dorothy Ann was suffering, when anything could be thought of to give her relief. And she should not mind any trouble in the use of the remedies, if only that dreadfully distressing pain could be kept at bay for a little while.

To which beautiful solicitude and sympathy Meta listened with a little surprise, never having heard Aunt Hacklebury's rheumatism exalted into such importance before. Indeed, in a general way it was rather ignored than otherwise at Percy Cottage. But Meta would know better in time. She would find that Dorothy Ann's aches and pains, when they kept her from going out to pay the bills, or order in the stores, or look after repairs, or get the dividends cashed, and those same aches and pains when wanted to keep her from going where sister Waldemar had not intended her to go, were by no means identical. Even rheumatism could be a convenience, in its way.

But, as Mrs. Waldemar said, an odd number was a nuisance in a small select party. Now, if only Meta and herself accepted Mrs. Ellesley's invitation, everything could be arranged as easily as possible. Meta would of course chat away with Mrs. Ellesley, the dear old lady seemed to have taken quite a fancy to her, whilst she herself would draw the Doctor out into a little interesting conversation, and perhaps succeed still further in putting him out of love with that monotony, which, of course, he never felt so much as when it came to be contrasted with the charm of such a companion as she could be when she chose.

So it was that Mrs. Waldemar and Meta, only they two, set off to the Carriden-Regis College on Monday afternoon, leaving Miss Hacklebury behind to a diet of knitting and meditation in the Percy Cottage dining-room. Miss Hacklebury, as she said herself, had no vocation for going out to tea; she rather disliked it than otherwise.

It was a charmingly successful little evening. Everything passed off as pleasantly as even Mrs. Waldemar herself could have wished. The Doctor was evidently delighted to see them. Mrs. Ellesley said, before he joined them at the tea-table, that he was very pleased when she told him, after Mrs. Waldemar's call the other day, of the arrangement she had made for Monday. He had mentioned it several times since, and expressed his hope that nothing would occur to prevent it from being carried out. And he had been quite anxious about the weather all day, and when the clouds began to threaten towards noon, he had proposed sending Bateson over with the pony-carriage, lest Mrs. and Miss Waldemar should be afraid of venturing on foot. Which anxiety Mrs. Waldemar was quite sure meant a great deal from a man like Dr. Ellesley, so exceedingly averse to society as his mother said he generally was, and so very glad when any excuse could be found for avoiding it. Mrs. Waldemar thought she knew why he had suddenly become so very sociably inclined, and it was the triumph induced by that knowledge which imparted such a glow to her cheek on this particular evening, and lent such an animated expression to her still beautiful dark eyes, and infused into her manner that charming consciousness of power and fascination, which, as people said, made her perfectly irresistible when she assumed it.

Perhaps it was that, too, which embolden- ed her to suggest, during the course of the evening, a stroll through the college grounds, on Meta's account. Meta really was develop- ing into a wonderful convenience.

" You know, Doctor, I *should* like her to see that beautiful view from the end of the beech-tree avenue. You were so kind as to take me there to see it when I called upon Mrs. Ellesley for the first time, and I was *so* enraptured. I told you, Meta, my pet, how enraptured I was, did I not? And she does *dote* so upon scenery, Dr. Ellesley, does this young daughter of mine. I often tell her she was born to be an artist's wife. I suppose I shall have her running away from me some day with a painter or something of that sort; and then she will have someone who can sympathise with her even more than I do myself, though I am sure I am quite foolish sometimes about the beauties of Nature. *Do* take us down the beech-tree avenue, Doctor."

To which the Doctor, nothing loth, for to be anywhere with Meta was happiness enough for him, replied by fetching his hat and then steering out towards the avenue, in his usual hazy, abstracted fashion, looking round now and then to see that the ladies were safe. Poor dear man! as Mrs. Waldemar thought to herself, what a treasure he would be in

a house, so delightfully ready to **do** anything
that anybody wanted him to do, scarcely
seeming to have a will of his own at all.
That was always the way with these very
talented people. They were so much easier
to manage in the house than your wide-
awake, shrewd, practical men of business,
who were always on the look-out for themselves and their own interests. There was
nothing like devotion to literary pursuits
for taking away a man's self-assertion, and
making him easy to live with.

But Mrs. Waldemar had no intention at
all that Meta should make the odd number
in that delightful little garden stroll. Accordingly, when the prospect had been duly
admired, and the garden praised as if there
was not such another paradise in existence,
and the Doctor congratulated upon the charming home which Providence had allotted to

him, she said, as if the thought had suddenly struck her,

"Beautiful! perfectly beautiful! But Meta, my darling—I am afraid—*don't* you think dear Mrs. Ellesley will feel lonely without us both? I should be *so* grieved for her to think we were neglecting her. It always distresses me so to appear to neglect any one, and I am so *very* much afraid she may be feeling lonely. Do you know, it never occurred to me until just this moment."

Mrs. Waldemar knew that would be enough. Away flew Meta, without any further hint or direction, back to the sofa where dear Mrs. Ellesley was resting, and stayed there all the rest of the evening, with her mamma's entire approval. After that she noticed that the Doctor was even more meditative and abstracted than before, and seemed to have more difficulty in bring-

ing his sentences to a prosperous termina-
tion. But that little circumstance was, of
course, quite natural. Indeed, it was rather
in her favour than otherwise, since it showed
a due sense of his position, and, at the
same time, a due sense of the difficulty
which a man like the Doctor would be sure
to feel in availing himself of it. If he had
been perfectly easy and self-possessed, if he
had chatted away with the fluency of an
accomplished squire of dames about the
weather and the scenery, and the forward-
ness of the season, and the unusual beauty
of the spring foliage, and so forth, without
a shade of nervousness or embarrassment,
Mrs. Waldemar would not have had half so
much faith in her ultimate assumption of
the queen-consortship, or queen-regnancy, as
she had privately determined it should be,

in the little kingdom of the Governor's establishment at Carriden-Regis College.

Meta's step-mamma was not more delighted to get her daughter hurried away than Meta herself was to be dismissed. Sitting by Mrs. Ellesley's side in the library, she felt, almost for the first time since she came home, the content of being with some one whom she could both trust and love. Already the emptiness of life at Percy Cottage was wearying her. Her own heart, honest and truthful, had begun to feel the want of like honesty and truthfulness in the graceful, lady-like woman in whose care—such care as it was—she was henceforth to find shelter. She had had but little experience of the world as yet, but that experience, until she came to Carriden-Regis, was all of gentleness and affection. Her life in that quiet south of England village had certainly not been of the most brilliant or varied. Her great-aunt, Miss Warrener, old and infirm, had been able to introduce her into but little society. She had had few "advantages," meaning thereby few opportunities of mingling in gay company, going to balls, quadrille-parties, and other similar places of amusement, where young ladies acquire the polish of fashionable life, and learn to school themselves into that self-possessed complacency which they consider the finishing touch of good breeding. But she had had what is perhaps worth more than these advantages, the companionship from childhood of a genuinely refined and pure-hearted woman; and this companionship had developed all that was best in her own nature, whilst it rendered her more sensitive to the want of refinement and perfect sincerity in those about her. Bear with it as she might, the glassy politeness of Mrs. Waldemar was very chilling. The substratum of base metal was beginning to wear up through its thin plating of silver. And as for Miss Hackle-bury, circumstances had not yet developed the vein of genuine true-heartedness which underlaid the exceedingly tough fibre of that good lady's external structure, so that Meta could scarcely tell what to make of her straightforward, matter-of-fact aunt. For the present, life at Percy Cottage could only be a congenial thing to her as she learned to forget what was best and truest in her own nature, and adapted herself to the super-ficial courtesy or undisguised bluntness of those about her.

With Mrs. Ellesley it was so different. With her Meta seemed to be breathing an entirely new atmosphere, or rather the old one which long habit had rendered so familiar. It was almost like being with Aunt Warrener again to look into that kind truthful face, and hear that gentle voice and feel her hand held in a clasp so warm and loving as none had given to it since she came home to Percy Cottage. Meta could have sat by Mrs. Ellesley's side all the evening, nor thought it long. There was such rest in feeling herself cherished and cared for again, after so long a spell of loneliness.

But she seemed to have been there only a very little while, when one of the servants came to the door.

"Is the Governor in, ma'am?"

"No, Ruth," said Mrs. Ellesley. "Who seeks him?"

"Mr. Garton, ma'am, wants to speak to him about a book for one of the professors."

"Tell Mr. Garton Dr. Ellesley is engaged just now with friends in the grounds. He will be at liberty directly, and then I will ask him about the book."

The servant was going away, when Mrs. Ellesley called her back, saying, as she did so, to Meta—

"My dear, I forgot; this Mr. Garton is the student you told me about; the one, you remember, who showed you the way through the wood. You can thank him now again, if you like. Ruth, ask Mr. Garton to come in and wait until Dr. Ellesley is at liberty. I daresay he will not be much longer in the grounds."

Stephen came in, in his thread-bare study-coat, his worn necktie,—not his calico sleeves, though, for he did not happen to have been writing,—his hair the reverse of tidy, a shabbily-bound book sticking from his pocket on one side, a bundle of Burton prize exercises on the other, just as he had turned out ·from a two hours' tug at mathematics in his little den upstairs. The evening shadows were beginning to creep up, and the heavy crimson curtains of the library-window kept out much of what little daylight still lingered, so that Stephen, when he first entered the room, saw no one there but Mrs. Ellesley.

"I am scarcely fit to come in," he said, stuffing the old book and the exercises further into his pocket, "only the professor who is reading with Charnock wants that geometry of his. I think, if you don't mind my meddling with the Governor's books, I can find it myself, without troubling anyone else."

And Stephen was turning towards the bookcase, which stood in the recess by the window, when, in doing so, he nearly stumbled over a young lady who was sitting on a footstool on the shady side of the sofa. He knew her again as soon as she came out into the twilight, looking up to him with the old bright smile and frank, pleasant voice. Only that now her little hand was reached out to take his, as Mrs. Ellesley said—

"Mr. Garton, Miss Waldemar. This is the young lady, Mr. Garton, who was indebted to you for guidance through the wood the other day. You see you guided her so well that she has been able to find the way again. If you are not very busy in your study, will you stay with us until the Governor comes?"

Was Stephen likely to be very busy in his study after that? So he stayed.

CHAPTER VI.

HALF an hour later, only half an hour, and yet it seemed like a whole long beautiful lifetime to Stephen Garton, sitting there in Meta's presence, treasuring up every word she uttered, printing every unconscious look upon his heart, the Governor and Mrs. Waldemar came in. Who says our sweetest moments pass most quickly? Nay, their very sweetness overflows all sense of time, and turns them, even as they pass, into a shoreless sea of golden, glorious memories. Stephen felt as if he had been gazing into the face of his Hermione for years and years, and yet only one little half hour had passed since first he clasped hands with her.

With a bright merry laugh Meta did the introduction herself, this time.

"Mamma, this is the Mr. Garton that I met in the wood. Now, do you think he looks like a vagabond, or a poacher, or anything of that sort? Mr. Garton, mamma says if she had met you alone in a wood, she should have been so frightened."

" Oh! Meta, my darling,"—and Mrs. Waldemar put out her two white hands with such a pretty deprecating gesture. She was in one of her sweetest, most triumphant moods to-night; that stroll in the College grounds had been so very delightful—" what a provokingly saucy little creature you are. Do not take any notice of what she says, Mr. Garton. I assure you it is only her nonsense. I don't think there ever was such a nonsensical little creature in the world as my pet Meta."

And then, turning to the Doctor with a fascinating smile, she asked,

"What *shall* I do with this naughty little girl of mine, Doctor, if she tells such tales of me? Only, you know, I *am* so easily frightened. I am sure if I had seen **Mr.** Garton I should have been ready to faint. I do so dread going out without anyone to take care of me. Though I daresay it is very foolish; it is such a thing, **you** know, to have such weak nerves; it does make one so helpless and dependent."

Then, gracefully wheeling round again in **Mr.** Garton's direction, she continued—

"And so, **Mr.** Garton, you are the gentleman who was so kind to my poor little Meta when she was in such distress, **and** could **not** find her way out of the wood?

So kind of you!—so *very* kind! And to walk so far with her yourself, too! Oh! it was so *very* good of you! Because, you know, if she really *had* lost her way—I declare it quite distresses me even to think about it now—I should never have forgiven myself, never, for allowing her to go into the wood alone. It was so good of you, Mr. Garton—so *very* good! I feel as if I could not thank you enough for taking so much trouble."

And Mrs. Waldemar shook hands with this Stephen Garton, Dr. Ellesley's most promising student, as she had heard he was, with as much impressiveness as though he had been the means of rescuing her daughter from a watery grave, or some other equally dreadful catastrophe.

Her eloquence produced the same effect upon Stephen as it had apparently done upon the Doctor, who was subsiding into his arm-chair with a crushed and altogether collapsed expression of countenance. However delightful that stroll in the College grounds might have been to Mrs. Waldemar, it had evidently produced a bewildering effect upon the Doctor's mind. With his lady companion's frequent references to her nervous system, and her touching reminiscences of bygone felicity, added to her pathetic lamentation upon the want of a kindred spirit, on none of which subjects the Doctor could command a proper amount of sympathy—he really had been almost overpowered. It was such a relief to get back into his arm-chair and be quiet; to look across now and then to Meta, gentle, peaceful little Meta, whose very face had a world of rest in it and happy memory for him, and to hear from time to time the sound of her voice, which, falling soft, sweet, and low, was like the last sunshiny drops of an April shower after the patter and commotion of the regular downfall has passed away. Mrs. Waldemar, however, did not appear to be disconcerted by the silence of the gentlemen. She prided herself on being able to sustain a conversation with ease and fluency. Indeed, she considered it a compliment, rather than otherwise, when, as a public speaker would say, she had the floor, and was allowed to expatiate at her own sweet will over whatever subjects self-interest might render desirable.

After the lights were brought in, she investigated Mr. Garton, put him through the sieve of scrutiny as regarded his accent, manner, personal appearance, and general abilities. Moreover, she watched the expression of his countenance whenever Meta

spoke; the eager interest—for Stephen was
not a man who could well conceal his feelings—with which he watched her every
movement and gesture, Dr. Ellesley, poor
dear man! looking into the fire all the time,
evidently absorbed in a sort of waking
dream. Mrs. Waldemar thought his dream
on this occasion most likely had something
to do with that stroll in the College
grounds. He had had something on his
mind during the whole time—she was quite
sure of that—something which, on account
of his extreme shyness and slowness of
speech, he could not bring himself to speak
out. Most likely anything of that kind
would be done by him in a letter. A letter on such a subject was a most admirable
resource for a shy man. Indeed, a *very*
shy man could scarcely do it in any other
way. Possibly he might be turning it over

in his own mind as he sat gazing into the fire in that extremely abstracted, meditative manner.

Nothing more was said about the book. Apparently Mrs. Ellesley had forgotten to tall her son why Mr. Garton had joined them in the library that night. And for Stephen there was but one book in all the world he cared to read just then.

When, after what Mrs. Waldemar called an hour of delightful social intercourse, the ladies rose to depart, Dr. Ellesley prepared, as in duty bound, to accompany them. So did Stephen Garton, encouraged thereto by Mrs. Waldemar, who had been plying him diligently with compliments and conversational attentions ever since she came into the room. Her investigation had evidently resulted favourably, judging from her extreme urbanity towards the subject of it.

And really it was astonishing in what numerous and unlooked-for ways Mrs. Waldemar could make herself agreeable when some ulterior motive, known only to herself, prompted her to it. It was almost impossible for anyone to resist that winning manner of hers, or to believe that all those sweetly pretty feminine graces were other than natural and ingrained to the woman who wore them with such charming ease.

But Mrs. Waldemar knew that Mr. Garton's escort for Meta would be a convenience, since it must of necessity leave Dr. Ellesley to herself for the whole of that long walk, nearly a mile and a half, if they went the shortest way, to Carriden-Regis. It was quite fortunate, she said to herself, that the young man happened to come in just when he did, and so prevent that nuisance of nuisances, a third party for the walk to Percy Cottage.

So they set out, sauntering leisurely, for the night was balmy and starlight. Just the night for sweet thoughts to blossom into speech, and for hopes that hid themselves from day's garish eye to breathe their fragrance as flowers do when the sun has gone. If Mrs. Waldemar expected, however, that the starlight would produce any such developing effects upon her extremely quiet and undemonstrative companion, she was mistaken. Their walk was as quiet as that other walk which the Doctor had taken a fortnight ago, with Meta by his side instead of Meta's step-mamma; and the same sweet thoughts, though not blossoming into speech, stirred within him now as then. It was little consequence to that calm, deep-lying, unwavering love of his, whether the woman to whom he gave it walked by his side or by another's side, for the present. He felt that she belonged to him, wherever she was, and feeling that, he could wait patiently until the time came for him to reach out his hand and take her to him for ever.

At last they reached Percy Cottage. Mrs. Waldemar had to pull the Doctor's sleeve, as Meta had had to pull it on a previous occasion, or he would have gone past the house.

"Are we here?" he asked, in reply to the gentle intimation. "I—I thought we had not come more than half way."

Mrs. Waldemar smiled complacently. It was just the very thing, under the circumstances, that he ought to think. Still, if he would say what he thought about other things than the distance to Percy Cottage, it would be desirable.

"So kind of you, Dr. Ellesley, so much obliged to you, Mr. Garton," she said, when they had separately declined her invitation to enter and rest. "Well, if you really *will* not come in, we must say good night to you here. I feel as if it was so very naughty of us to have given you all this trouble; but you see, having no gentleman at Percy Cottage, makes such a difference. In poor dear Mr. Waldemar's time, I should never have had to trespass upon my friends for such an attention as this. And *do* tell dear Mrs. Ellesley what a delightful evening we have had, and how *very* much we have enjoyed it, and how *very* much obliged we are to her; so kind of her, such a delicious change. And so glad too for dear Meta's sake, for you know I am so anxious for her to have a little congenial society; a little congenial society, you know, is such a very improving thing for a young girl, now is it not, Dr. Ellesley?"

Dr. Ellesley said he did not know, perhaps it might be.

"Ah! you see that is always the way with you grand literary people. You have such resources within yourselves, you don't know what it is to want congenial society; but I assure you it *is* a need, you don't know what a need it is with some people. And pray, Mr. Garton, *do* come in and see us when you stroll over to the village. I am sure you must very often stroll over, and we should be so *delighted* to see you. Dear Mrs. Ellesley has told us *all* about you, I assure you she has, and I cannot tell you how *very* much interested I feel. I do so *dote* upon talent, Mr. Garton. There is nothing in the *world* I dote upon so much as talent. I have a perfect woman's

weakness for it. And so now, *do* call whenever you come to the village, and be sure
you don't forget. I shall say you are so
very naughty if you go away and forget."

And Mrs. Waldemar shook her head play-
fully at Mr. Garton. To tell her friends that
they were "very naughty," was the ex-
tremest length of maliciousness to which
her feminine gentleness ever allowed her to
go. And she used to say it to them as
though she thought it quite impossible that
they could ever have the hardihood to resist
such a threat, or, at any rate, not to escape
from it with all convenient speed.

So these two men, Stephen Garton and
Fergus Ellesley, went home again, side by
side, to the college of Carriden-Regis, there
to dream each his own dreams, and to pray,
each for his own happiness, if our own hap-

piness is a blessing for which we may ever dare to pray. These two men, either of whose life-palace must be built on the ruins of the other's; either of whose joy could only win its full crown and completeness by the wreck of the other's. For one of them to live contentedly with the woman he had chosen for himself, the other must travel alone and uncomforted for the rest of the journey. For one to hear the sweet bells of hope always chiming on his path, the other must be content to listen only to those of memory.

CHAPTER VII.

THAT evening's visit to the new dissent-
ing college of Carriden-Regis had sup-
plied Mrs. Waldemar with a fresh field for
planning and contriving. Stephen Garton,
though not exactly a gentleman in her own
sense of the word, not quite so stylish and
conversational and distinguished as she could
like, would be a very suitable match for
Meta. If she had any discernment in such
matters, and she thought she had as much
as other people, if not more, his own heart
was set upon something of the same kind.
Mrs. Ellesley hinted, when speaking of him,
that he had struggled with early difficulties;

meaning by that, of course, that his connections were not brilliant. Everybody knew what struggling with early difficulties meant, when spoken of in that way. Still, connections were not everything; indeed they were very little when a young man had the world before him, and such talent as Stephen Garton had already developed, to enable him to make his way in it.

Then, if he gained this Burton prize in September, and Mrs. Ellesley said he would be almost certain to gain it, none of the other competitors having anything like the amount of energy and perseverance which he could put forth when he chose, he was made for life. After he had returned from his Continental studies, and finished his college course, there was nothing for him to do but accept an invitation to some wealthy, respectable congregation, or very possibly become, in course of a few years, one of the professors in the Carriden-Regis College itself, with Meta for a wife.

Nothing could be more straightforward and satisfactory. Meta would make such an admirable minister's wife. Indeed, she seemed as if she were born to the position. She was so simple and unworldly, had so little notion of style or fashion, or any sort of gaiety. Mrs. Waldemar thought she might almost say she was unfit for anything else; a really brilliant position would be quite thrown away upon her, because she could not appreciate it, nor fill it properly. Such a character was sweetly pretty, but it never got a girl on in the world. What should she herself have been now, if she had had no more notion of contriving and managing and looking after her own interests than Meta appeared to have? A second-rate shopkeeper's wife most likely, living in a back parlour, keeping a small girl to help with rough work, and doing all the rest herself, perhaps coming into the shop on market days to attend to customers, and all that sort of thing; instead of mixing, as she did, with the very best society of the place, and being looked up to by the wives of professional men, and having Lady Fitzflannerly's card on the top of her basket in the drawing-room. There was nothing like contrivance and management and self-help for a woman, in such matters as these. And therefore, considering the very limited gifts which Meta possessed in that department, she might think herself fortunate in having attracted the attention of such a promising young man as Stephen Garton, who, if his antecedents were not all that could be wished, had at any rate made a fair start in the world, and could look forward to as good a position as most young men of his age.

Yes, Stephen Garton would do very well. Besides, when the Governor knew that Meta was finally disposed of, or likely to be, one great obstacle to his own domestic arrangements would be removed. It would make all the difference in the world to her, Mrs. Waldemar, as regarded her prospects of success in that direction, if Dr. Ellesley could be given to understand, before long, that Meta would not in any way interfere with his establishment, that she was already provided for in a suitable manner. And what manner could be more suitable than this? In what way could Mrs. Waldemar— she thought—more admirably fulfil her duties as a conscientious step-mamma, than by facilitating the happiness of these two young people, and securing for her daughter a comfortable settlement in life? Because that she had made an impression on Mr. Garton was quite evident, and all that was needed now was a little judicious management in the contriving of opportunities whereby that impression might be deepened.

A pleasant social intercourse must now therefore be established with Mr. Garton; a sort of friendship which, without exciting gossip at first, might place in his way abundant facilities for improving his acquaintance with Meta.

And here a happy thought struck Mrs. Waldemar. Mrs. Goverly, the wife of poor dear Mr. Waldemar's successor in the practice, had two little boys for whom she was desirous of meeting with a Latin tutor, the governess who at present had charge of them not being competent to impart instruction in classics. Mr. Garton would be the

very person for them. They could not have
a better teacher, as far as that went, and
old Mrs. Ellesley had said that Mr. Garton
wished to fill up his spare time as much
as possible in private teaching, his friends
not being able to render him much pecuniary assistance for the carrying out of his
college studies. She would step over to
Mrs. Goverly that very day, and mention
the subject to her; and if, as was most
likely—for the new solicitor's wife, looking
on Mrs. Waldemar in the light of a lady
patroness, and having been introduced by
her to some of the best society in the place,
seldom thought of contradicting anything
which she proposed—if, as was most likely,
Mrs. Goverly decided to avail herself of such
a favourable opportunity, she, Mrs. Waldemar,
would write a note to Mr. Garton at once,
requesting him to come over to Percy Cot-

tage, when she would introduce him to his new pupils.

Then, of course, when Mr. Garton was teaching in the village, it would be the most natural thing in the world—Mrs. Waldemar having been the means of procuring him that teaching—that he should step in to see her now and then, and take a quiet cup of tea with her, after the lessons were over. No one, not even Mrs. Danesborough, who was always so very ready with her tongue, could find fault with such a perfectly innocent arrangement as that. It would be charming, and just the very thing for dear Meta, the girl having such a foolish aversion to visiting or putting herself forward at all in general society, as other girls did.

Then, as Mrs. Ellesley had said that Mr. Garton always stayed at the college during vacation time, for the purpose of carrying on his studies, he would continue his teaching throughout the whole of the summer, so that it would be quite the young man's own fault if, with the facilities she intended to put in his way, he did not secure something advantageous for himself before long.

Though, perhaps, it would be as well for her not to allow anything like a formal engagement until after this affair of the scholarship was settled. Because, if by any unforeseen chance, young Garton *should* be thrown out, he would have as it were to begin the world again, and fight his way up through all the difficulties of an inferior position ; without the spur of hope, too, which, so long as the prize was yet uncertain, would keep him up to almost any exertion. A great deal more than money and honour would be lost if he missed that prize. He would lose heart and energy and vigour. He would be content with a second-rate position, he would dwindle down into a mere commonplace individual, to say nothing of the length of ·time which must then elapse before he could, with any sort of propriety, think of settling in life.

And to have Meta on her hands for three or perhaps four years, would be anything but desirable. A long engagement was a thing she could not endure, even when other circumstances did not render it so un-advisable as in the present case. Long en-gagements invariably came to nothing, and then a girl had, as it were, to begin the world again; just as young Garton would have to begin it again if he missed the Burton scholarship. No; she would just hold the affair in abeyance until September, and then, if all did turn out well, Mr. Garton would be at liberty to bring matters to a crisis. If not, the acquaintance might be dropped on some excuse or other, and a more eligible partner sought for Meta.

Mrs. Waldemar was admirably prompt when she once saw the game clearly laid out before her.

The day after that visit to the College, she called upon Mrs. Goverly, and represented to that lady in such glowing terms the advantages which would be gained by a superior Latin teacher for the little boys, that the solicitor's wife, to whom Mrs. Waldemar's will in all social arrangements was law, placed the matter entirely in her lady patroness's hands, authorising her to engage Mr. Garton on his own terms, and to fix such time as should be convenient to himself for his visits.

A note was then sent to Stephen, requesting him to call at Percy Cottage, Mrs. Waldemar being desirous of a little conversation with him respecting a lady who was looking out for classical instruction for her two boys. And on the day week of Garton's introduction to Meta's step-mamma, he was installed as private tutor to the little Goverlies, with the understanding that, whenever he could make it convenient to do so, he was to step in and take a cup of tea at Percy Cottage; his time at Ivy Lodge having been so disposed by Mrs. Waldemar, that the lessons should expire at a suitable period of the afternoon.

Furthermore, that Dorothy Ann, on whom the trouble of housekeeping devolved, should not rebel at this prospect of chance company dropping in at any time, sister Waldemar, who could be delightfully obliging when she chose, assured her that Mr. Gar-

ton being a young man who was not accustomed to much display, it would be quite
unnecessary to take the pea-green china
down when he came, or unwrap the best
silver teapot, or disinter the fine damask
table-cloths from their tomb in the great
chest at the top of the stairs, or indeed put
forth any of the manifestations of honour
which were usually brought into exercise at
Percy Cottage when visitors stayed to tea.
His friends lived in a very quiet way, in
fact, they were not in a position quite equal
to his own, and she only asked the young
man at all out of kindness, pure kindness,
being anxious to give him the opportunity
of a little pleasant society; for she had
heard that he was very deserving, and
worked hard to keep himself from being a
burden to the family.

And Mrs. Waldemar said there was nothing she admired in a young man so much as independence. It was so very praiseworthy, and she really thought that any one who was making such efforts as young Garton was making to get on in the world, ought to have every encouragement that people in a little better class of society could give him. Indeed, Mrs. Ellesley had told her that they considered every kindness shown to young Garton as shown to themselves, because her son felt such an almost fatherly interest in him, and was so very anxious for his welfare. And considering how very kind Dr. and Mrs. Ellesley had been to herself and Meta, she thought the least they could do was to try and make some return for it by reaching out a little courtesy towards anyone in whom the Governor felt interested.

That was how Mrs. Waldemar put it.

And sister Dorothy Ann, who had been very much mollified by that arrangement about the pea-green china, replied—

"Very well, sister Waldemar. The young man can come whenever you have a mind to."

CHAPTER VIII.

FOR Dorothy Ann Hacklebury was a really good-hearted woman, if only people found the right side of her, if only they did not set off with the impression, and give her to understand they had it too, that she was hard and rough and impracticable. It was that that soured her. It was that which made her get on badly in a general way with sister Waldemar. Sister Waldemar was always taking it for granted that she was a domestic tyrant, always professing to be in such implicit subjection to her—though all the time it was sister Hacklebury who did the subjection—and pretend-

ing to be so desperately afraid of giving
offence in the least little trifle. Whereas it
was as hard to offend Dorothy Ann Hacklebury as to offend a horse-chesnut when its
rind and spines are in full vigour. She
might be wounded, very often she was, by
people who did not understand her; she
might be put out, as Buttons put her out
fifty times a day, by leaving the side pas-
sage door on the latch; she might be
vexed by those everlasting nerves of sister
Waldemar's, and occasionally give vent to
something like a demonstration of impatience
concerning them; but as for being offended,
and sulking over the offence, and standing
on her dignity accordingly, and making
everybody else feel that something was
wrong with her, that was what Miss Hacklebury never did.

Moreover, she was very kindly disposed

in her way, although it was "an uncommon queer kind of way," as Buttons used to say, after being subjected to a severer diet of scolding than usual. If there was an act of self-denial to be done, Miss Hacklebury always did it, without so much as seeming to know that there was any merit in the doing of it, or loudly proclaiming her readiness to spend and be spent in the service of other people. She did a great deal of good with very little talk about it. When sister Waldemar was taken with the spasms, which event always happened in the dead of night, and when there chanced to be an unusually vicious east wind, it was sister Hacklebury who turned out of bed without a murmur, and went downstairs for bran bags and hot-water applications, and did the rubbing and the bathing and the chafing and the fomenting and everything else that needed to be done, and listened with the most impenetrable patience to her sister's pathetic invocations of the late poor dear Mr. Waldemar, who used to wait upon his beloved like an angel, and was so deliciously sympathising, and knew to a drop how much sal-volatile to give her. She should never meet with anyone again, she was sure she shouldn't, who could sympathise with her spasms like poor dear Mr. Waldemar. Just as much as to say that sister Dorothy Ann, standing over her in her flannel dressing-gown, shivering in the dim candlelight, did not understand them at all, and had no sort of gift worth being thankful for in the administration of sympathy or sal-volatile.

But Dorothy Ann did not care a bit for that, neither would she have cared if sister Waldemar had been twice as contrary, or received her ministrations with a more fractional amount of gratitude. It was her duty to get up when the spasms came on, and she did it; for she had a downright Spartan reverence for duty, a great deal more reverence for duty than for the attendant state of mental exaltation which some people assume when they have done it.

If Buttons, too, managed to catch a cold —and really the girl was always catching one in some way or other, although she looked like an Alpine mule for strength and toughness—it was Dorothy Ann who rummaged out the recipe-book, and cooked up such delicious possets of treacle, and honey, and sugar, and butter, and sallied into the kitchen a dozen times a day to dole out the same in spoonsful to Buttons, wondering how it was that the mixture took so little effect, when it had been given to her by her dear mother as a sovereign specific, warranted to cure the most obstinate cold or catarrh in twenty-four hours at the very least. Just as if Buttons, with all her mulish obtuseness, did not know a great deal better than to let her cold be over-speedily cured by such delightful posset as that, accompanied as it was every night by spiced gruel, and every morning by a cup of hot tea before she got up, to prevent the damp air from striking into her.

No, Dorothy Ann was really and genuinely kind, only the kindness being, as Buttons remarked, sometimes of an "uncommon queer sort," people did not always give her credit for it.

Perhaps one reason of this might be that so little sympathy mingled with it. Kind-heartedness and sympathy are two widely different qualities, though most people speak of them as one and the some thing. For many men, and some women, too, who are positively running over with benevolence and good-will, have not so much as a fibre of that fine, delicate perception which enables them to take knowledge of the needs, sorrows, sicknesses, and sufferings of the inner life, or lay any sweet touch of healing upon them.

Sister Dorothy Ann was admirably benevolent. She would have gone to the farthest end of the village, at any hour of the day or night, and at any expense of personal inconvenience, to take lint and plaster to a child which had had the misfortune to tumble into the fire and almost burn itself to death. And she would have applied them, too, with quick-handed neatness such as a hospital-nurse might envy; but all the time that she was doing so she would have been scolding the little urchin for his mis-

chievousness in going near the fire when
mother was out; and even whilst she was
stuffing mint lozenges into his mouth to stop
his crying, she would have looked down upon
him with a hard common-sense face which
seemed to say,

"I told you so. See what naughty children get for not minding what their mothers
tell them."

Or she would sit up half the night, fomenting Buttons' sprained ankle, lecturing her
meanwhile with vigorous volubility for having
been so stupid as to get it sprained with
going, two steps at a time, down the cellar-
steps, and when she had been told, too, over
and over again, never to think of doing such
a thing. It was carelessness, nothing but
carelessness, and she deserved everything she
got for not paying more attention to what
was said to her, and it was a mercy every

bone in her body wasn't broken, instead of having just a sprained ankle to remember her disobedience by.

And then Miss Hacklebury used to tuck her up in bed, and give her some nice warm drink to send her to sleep, and tramp down the cold uncarpeted attic stairs to her own room again.

Admirable woman! practical and sensible in the extreme. But she could not listen ten minutes to a tale of grief for which there was not some actual tangible remedy in the shape of liniment or embrocation. Her skill was all for the body. She had none, or very little, in ministering to a mind diseased, wearied, oppressed, cast down with the little cares and worries of daily life. Just so much of human ill as could be cured by herb tonics and external applications, Miss Hacklebury would willingly spend her time in curing.

What could not be reached by these, lay, for the most part, beyond her ken.

Here, however, was a definite act of kindness to be done to this young man, and Dorothy Ann did it with hearty good-will; and the more so because his coming in from time to time for a cup of tea, as sister Waldemar proposed he should come in, by way of showing respect to Dr. Ellesley, did not involve the taking down and dusting of the pea-green china, nor the upheaving of the linen-chest in quest of suitably fine damask cloths.

He was a minister, too. At least, if he was not a minister now, he was going to be made one as soon as he had finished his divinity course; and if Miss Hacklebury ever *did* feel herself drawn out towards one person more than another, it was towards a minister. She always had respected the

ministerial office, and she always meant to
do so, and if it was for nothing more than
his prospects in that line, Mr. Garton should
be welcome every time he came, to an extra
spoonful of their best black tea, and an
exceptionally liberal allowance of buttered
crumpet, which was her idea of show-
ing honour to the ministerial office. She
couldn't converse, she used to say, like
sister Waldemar; she couldn't fascinate people
by the charms and graces of her personal
behaviour; she couldn't, by any amount of
careful dressing, make herself an object of
attraction, so far as her outer woman was
concerned, and so minister delight to anyone who came to the house; but she *could*
send up as good a dish of tea as the
handsomest woman in Carriden-Regis, and
supplement it, too, with as tempting an
array of home-made cakes; for no one could

deny that she had as light a hand at baking as even a born and bred pastry-cook;
and sometimes even ministers, who were the
only people she cared to honour, appreciated
these things as much as fine conversation
and a prepossessing personal appearance.

But if Miss Hacklebury dealt kindly with
Stephen Garton at first for his calling's
sake, she learned to esteem him by-and-by
for his own. She had strong prejudices.
When she disliked anybody she did it
heartily, and when she "took to them," as
she expressed it, she did that just as heartily.
Perhaps Stephen Garton reminded her of
someone towards whom, in her younger
days, she had cherished a maidenly preference. Perhaps a long time ago, a very long
time ago, before Miss Hacklebury fell into
what people called "those very odd ways
of hers," before she gave over trying to

dress herself nicely, and before that hard, rigid, determinate look came into her face, she, too, had had a little romance, gilding the earlier years of a life over which stern common-sense now reigned supreme. She, too, might have been conscious of a thrill at that heart, now so very steady-going and matter-of-fact, when some young man, like this student, Stephen Garton, came in occasionally in an evening to the little_ back parlour behind the shop, and glanced tenderly, and said sweet things to her when there was no one near to listen. And sent valentines, too—for it was never sister Dorothy Ann who scolded Buttons for receiving valentines—and wrote love-letters to her when she went away from home. And perhaps if Miss Hacklebury's romance had not been nipped in the bud; if fate, or fortune, or that other thing which men miscall chance, had not been untoward, that hard determined look would never have come upon her face, and she would never have fallen into what people called "those very odd ways of hers," and she would never have given up what a loved and loving woman clings to so long, the desire to make herself look nice.

However that might be, Miss Hacklebury took to Stephen Garton very kindly, and always made tea from the best side of the caddy when he came, and instructed Joanna not to spare the crumpets, or send them in to the room scant of butter, as that thrifty person was apt to do when the family were by themselves. And after one or two visits had fostered a comfortable degree of intimacy between them, she offered to mend his gloves, or set a button on them; and she told him that if ever he wanted a pocket-handkerchief hemming, or anything of that sort, and being so far away from home, it might not always be convenient to send it there, she should be very glad to do it for him. She rather liked having someone to do for, she said, and be kind to, though people *did* seem to think she was a crooked old stick, good for nothing but to do the scolding of the house.

At last, when he had been to tea three or four times, Miss Hacklebury said to her sister—

"Sister Waldemar, I mean to knit that young man a set of stockings. It strikes me his friends don't look after him very much, to make him very comfortable, and if he goes to Germany, as Mrs. Ellesley says he's likely to, on account of the scholarship, they'll be a great advantage to him. There's nothing like hand-wrought stockings for comfort, especially if they're wrought by a person that has a liking for you; and I've taken to that young man uncommonly ever since he began to come to the house. I don't know why I should, but I have. My dear mother used to say there's nothing you knit kindness into like a pair of stockings; they're better for comfort than the best that money can buy. I'll get some worsted in the village, and set a pair on this very night."

And so she did, and Meta wound the yarn for her.

CHAPTER IX.

THEN came the beautiful, beautiful summer, so warm, so balmy, so golden.
Old people who had lived in Carriden-Regis
all their lives, said they had never seen a
summer like it before. For the sun rose
morning after morning with never a cloud
about him, and set in a splendour of purple and gold, which poured down upon the
great brown Millsmany moors, steeping them
in a glow as of cloudland itself, and which
struck in quivering sparkles upon the windows of St. Wilfred's Church, making the
old tower look as though crusted over with
many-coloured gems. And never had the

roses blossomed so bravely, nor the honey-
suckle trailed such wealth of perfumed gar-
lands over the green hedgerows, nor the
white cherry blossom fallen to give place
to such clusters of luscious crimson fruit,
nor the apricots on those old-mossed walls
which enclosed the Manor-house garden,
showed such downy promise of sweetness
hidden behind their green leaves. And never
had the wildflowers blossomed with such
wild luxuriance in Carriden-Regis wood,
covering every glade of it with a tesse-
lated pavement, whose like for richness and
beauty no Eastern mosque or temple ever
showed. And never had the birds sung so
merrily, nor the nightingale told his tale
from branches where the hawthorn bloomed
in such white bridal splendour. It was a
summer amongst a thousand, that it was,
as the old men said, loitering at evening

time on the village green, while the shadows
lengthened and the sun-gleams quivered in
streaks and patches of gold among the beech-
tree leaves.

For Stephen Garton, too, there never had
been such a summer before. The summer
of the year and the summer of his life
came hand-in-hand to him. All the toil
that had gone before, all the weariness, all
the waiting, were remembered no more than
now, in the flowery June-time, he remembered the chill bitter winds and the grey
rack and mist which had kept the sunlight
away from him. They lay far behind him,
parted from him by the golden gate of love,
through which he passed that afternoon when
Meta Waldemar first spoke to him.

With what new ardour he toiled on now
for that place in the world where he hoped
not to stand alone. How short those long

hours of study seemed, for each brought
him nearer to that goal which, having
reached, he might, a poor man and mean
no longer, hold out his hand to clasp hers.
Rodney Charnock's jeers, those vexing taunts
which had rankled so bitterly in his memory once, how little, how trivial they
seemed now to him, who had hidden away
in his heart, far down beneath any power
of theirs to reach it, a well-spring of hope,
pure and fresh and undefiled. Ah! he could
afford to smile and be patient over them.
Nay, that they were given him at all, only
made the brightness which they could not
touch, seem brighter.

Stephen came three times a week into
Carriden-Regis to give lessons to the little
Goverlies. He had some teaching in Millsmany, too, to which he went on the alter-
nate days, so that he was able to keep

himself now without drawing on his poor old mother's resources. After this work was done, and his classes attended, and his questions got up for the Burton examination, there was not much time for rest, not much time for castle-building, even though the castles could be made so beautiful now.

The professors said he was working too hard. He could not stand it long, they said. He would have to give up some day, break down, perhaps pay with the loss of life itself, at any rate with the loss of health and energy, for that prize which would then be so dearly bought.

Stephen knew better. It was no hard work for him. He had no weariness, he felt no pain, for the sweet hope which had sprung up within him had overflowed all his life, as the Nile its parched and thirsty banks, with strength and richness and plenty. What was labour to him with the great thought of Meta's love to lighten it? What were those long hours of toil in study and class-room if week by week·he could put between them and him the memory of her smile, the hope of some bright, encouraging word of hers? And how little would· ten times that drudgery of daily teaching have seemed, so long as it brought him nearer to her, so long as it was done for her sweet sake?

Then, in the sultry summer afternoons, when thought grew drowsy, and the tired brain asked leave to rest for awhile from Greek and science and mathematics, Stephen would go into the Carriden-Regis wood and tread his way over the moss and creepers to that fallen trunk, almost buried now in the midst of a great cluster of brackens, where he was sitting when for the first time he met Meta Waldemar. And then, while the warm sunshine quivered and gleamed round every leaf, and the soft warm breath of June stole up the scented glades, he would live over again all the happy past, and revel in thoughts of a happier future; that sweet smile of hers the sun alike of future and past, Meta's face looking out upon him from every flower, Meta's voice speaking to him in every bird-note, Meta's fingers touching his in every little leaflet that the wind stirred around him. Happy June days, each giving him some new joy, each translating into brighter memory what had once been such bright hope, each show-ing him more and more of the glory and the beauty and the richness of the life whose light is given from above.

After the College broke up in the early

part of the month, Dr. Ellesley went away, as he generally did in the summer time, to Geneva, where he had many acquaintances amongst the literati and professors of the university there. The students dispersed to their respective homes, leaving only Stephen behind to tug away at competition work. Rodney Charnock returned to the bosom of his family at Carriden-Regis, there to study, as he said, for the examination; although, from the frequency with which he was to be met, in company with his sister Belle, at the Millsmany flower-shows, regattas, cricket-matches, promenade concerts, and other town gaieties, the studies were not carried on with painful assiduity.

Mrs. Waldemar, also, took the opportunity, no further operations being possible at the College, of going from home and paying a round of visits amongst her friends, intending to finish the series by a tolerably long sojourn with old Mr. Waldemar, her late dear husband's uncle, the venerable bachelor from whose demise, even yet, some advantageous pecuniary results might possibly arise. Meta was left at home under the guardianship of Miss Hacklebury.

Those were wonderfully quiet, happy days for Percy Cottage. Buttons, who had never known it before, in Mrs. Waldemar's absence, said the place was not like itself for peace and comfort. There were no more hysterics, no more nervous attacks, no more summoning of poor Buttons to dust the parlour at such times as Gibbs, the milkman's boy, was coming up the back-garden with a view to a little private conversation; or banishing of her upstairs when the fascinating grocer from Millsmany came for his weekly orders. Even Miss Hacklebury's temper seemed to take a turn when sister Waldemar went away. Or perhaps it might be that the east wind having ceased to infest the premises, that worthy lady's patience was not so severely tried by the banging of the doors, and the careering of unfriendly gusts of air through the passages. At any rate, an unwonted spirit of peace and quietness seemed to settle down upon the house as soon as Mrs. Waldemar, with her retinue of trunks and band-boxes, was safely *en route* for Millsmany station.

Miss Hacklebury continued her kindly offices towards Stephen Garton. He was an estimable young man, she said, with no nonsense about him, and so she told him that she should be glad to see him, now that sister Waldemar was away, all the same as when she was at home. Indeed, if he liked to come in and have his tea any afternoon when he was teaching in the village, there would always be a cup and saucer ready for him. Only she hoped he wouldn't stay late at nights. She couldn't bear people staying late at nights. It always put her about so. It was a peculiarity she had inherited from their dear father. When he had retired from business, and they lived in the small house at Poplarcroft, the servant always came in at nine o'clock, let who might be there, and put the shutters up, and laid the Bible on the table, ready for worship; and if the visitors did not see then that it was time to go, her dear father used to tell them the fact in so many words. He was a man that never hesitated about speaking his mind, was her dear father. And that was how she should like to do if she was mistress at Percy Cottage, only sister Waldemar did not approve it. There were a good many things in which she and sister Waldemar did not see eye to eye. But if Mr. Garton did not object to that little peculiarity of hers—she knew it was a peculiarity—about visitors going home early, he might come to the house as often as he had a mind to.

Sister Dorothy Ann did not care for the men a bit, as she always used to say when Mrs. Waldemar deplored the lack of congenial masculine society in the village of Carriden-Regis. For her part, she had gone along through life very well without them, and she did not see any use in the fuss that sister Waldemar always made when a gentleman happened to drop in to tea; getting out the best china, and setting the silver cake-basket in the middle of the table, and putting in the fire in the drawing-room, and stripping off the covers from the worked chairs, just to make him believe that they lived in their best rooms and used their best things every day of their lives. For her part she thought people always saw through anything of that kind. She was never able to carry it off naturally herself. She always *did* feel anxious when the best china was out, and she couldn't help, however much sister Waldemar frowned and winked at her for doing it, cautioning Buttons to be careful when she carried the cups round, and turning to watch her until she got the tray fairly out at the door, lest she should catch her sleeve in the handle, or something of that sort. And she always lifted the cake-basket off the table herself, though sister Waldemar told her it was very vulgar to do so, and put it away into the cupboard. She would rather be vulgar than have Buttons break the handle by seizing upon it in her rough, boisterous fashion. People ought not to have such

things as those, uuless they had proper servants to look after them; and if they had
not proper servants, why, then, let it be
vulgar, or let it be what it might, she
could not help feeling it on her mind to
give an eye to them herself, no matter who
was there to take notice.

And as for making such a fuss about
gentlemen visitors, as sister Waldemar always used to make, Miss Hacklebury had
never seen any man for a good many years,
never indeed since before their dear father
retired from the grocery business, who, when
he came up the street, made her feel as if
she should like to run upstairs and put on
a more becoming gown, and slip off her
old head-dress or anything of that sort.
They were a poor set, were the men, for
the most part now-a-days, and if the women
could get along without them, they had

better do it. For take the best of them
that ever you might, they required a great
deal of pleasing, and never could be exactly
suited about their dinners, and were fit to
carry the roof off the house if their meals
were not sent up to the minute. A woman
had a great deal to bear with when she
took one in hand to do for and look after.
That was *her* opinion.

And as for supporting a woman's weakness, and standing stiff and upright like an
iron pillar, or an apple-tree stump, or an
oak-post for her to cling to, that sounded
very well in poetry, but it fell to pieces
sadly when you went into real life with it.
She had been in a good many families in her
time, and she had seen several varieties of
domestic life, one way and another, as she
tramped up and down the world; and so far
as her observation went, she thought that

when a man married, he did not marry for the sake of having some one to support, but to set his buttons on and see that his meals were sent in regularly; and if she did not do that for him, it was precious little he cared for having her "cling" to him, as the poetry books said.

But still, though she didn't care for the men herself a bit, and would sooner be without them now than not, she had no objection to other people thinking differently if they chose. She could remember the time when she liked a little of that sort of thing herself. There was somebody once a long time ago, just before their dear father retired from the business—but, however, it was no use thinking about that now.

And then Miss Hacklebury would rattle away with such determinate energy at those stockings which she was knitting for Stephen

Garton, knitting them with such hearty good will, and putting into them so much downright womanly kindness, because Stephen's face had a look in it that reminded her of a young man she once knew, dead and buried more than thirty years ago. That memory, far off, but fresh and tender still, was the secret of much of Miss Hacklebury's unselfish consideration for other people. That was why she never sent Buttons out of the way when the grocer's young man was coming from Millsmany, and why she never went to the door herself when the postman knocked on Valentine's morning. She remembered that when she had valentines, and she did have very pretty ones once, she always liked to have time to stuff them into her pocket before any one else saw them. It seemed to take half their sweetness away if other people pounced upon them first. She had no

doubt Buttons and Joanna had feelings somewhat similar. She did not know that they
were any worse for having them. She did
not know that she was any better, any
holier, any purer, now that all these things
were swept out of her heart, leaving it
empty and untenanted, save by those who
came out or went in as they listed. She
used to say her prayers as earnestly when
she was a young girl, with a love-letter
hidden away in the bosom of her dress, as
ever she said them now that that love-
letter had lain for thirty years, yellow, stained, mouldering, in her writing-desk. And
she was willing that others should find, and
keep if they could, the joy which had once
been given to her for such a brief season;
just given to keep one little spot in the
garden of her heart green and fresh until
death's winter came, and after that winter the
everlasting spring.

And so sometimes in an evening, when Stephen Garton had come in to tea, as he generally did come in once a week, if not oftener, she would find something to do out of the room. She had some very fine laces to iron that could not be trusted to any but her own hands; or Buttons had been leaving some of the doors on the latch, and must be spoken to about it; or she suddenly remembered a note that she must write to sister Waldemar, sister Waldemar would think they were neglecting her if she did not get a note next morning; or she disappeared into the store-room in search of herb bags to prepare some decoction or other for Jane Gubston, the sexton's wife, whose liver that summer was in a chronic state of disarrangement, and who never felt so much relief from any doctor's stuff as from Miss Hacklebury's dandelion. And, once

out of the room, she did not particularly
hurry back again, thinking that the young
people would get on very well without her.

For she had watched Stephen Garton's
eyes, how they followed Meta about, how
a warm misty light quivered in them when
they met hers, how his voice took a tenderer
tone when he spoke to her, how his hand
trembled if hers did but chance to touch it.
And she had noticed a change come over
Meta too. First of all the faintest little
touch of saucy independence had marked
her behaviour to Stephen Garton, just such
an independence as she remembered feeling
herself a long time ago, when somebody
began to be particularly attentive to her;
a touch of maiden freedom that would not
at once, and without a struggle, give in even
to love's gentle restraint. Then there came
a changeful look into the young girl's face,

sometimes happy, sometimes restless, the shining out of a light within that was not the old, quiet light of perfect peace and content. And she knew—for though people called her hard, there was a little kernel of sweetness beneath the rough cocoa-nut fibre of her disposition—that these two young hearts were quivering towards each other, and by-and-by they would meet and touch and commingle, never, she hoped, to part any more. For if there was one thing in the world which made Dorothy Ann Hacklebury sad, and not many things *could* make her sad, it was the parting, through wrong, mischance, misunderstanding, or deceit of others, of two hearts which did really and truly belong to each other.

But she never spoke a word, never called up a blush on Meta's cheek, in Stephen's presence or out of it, by any mysterious hints and allusions, or sly inuendoes which might brush the innocent bloom from thoughts so pure, true, and maidenly. For with all her hard, stringy practicality, there was not a particle of coarseness in Miss Hacklebury's nature. Perhaps many a fine lady, sailing about in the best London society, many a spoiled darling of fashion who never set foot in a kitchen in her life, and knew no more of baking or breadmaking than the great Mogul, would have been vastly the better for a little of that womanly propriety, that fine instinct of self-respect and respect for others which circumstances struck, like pure sparks out of flint, from Miss Hacklebury's externally hard and unloveable nature. At any rate she could do one thing which not many lookers-on, especially women, can do with regard to that sweet human secret —the dawn of love between soul and soul; she could hold her peace.

CHAPTER X.

MRS. WALDEMAR continued that summer diet of visiting amongst her friends, being duly informed from time to time of the health and well-being of those she had left behind at Percy Cottage. Her own let-ters were very full of protestations of affection to darling Meta, and longings for the time when she should return to pet and caress her. It was such a privation, she said, not having anyone to pet and caress. But at the same time she had not the slightest intention of putting the longings into any practical form until shortly before the time appointed for the opening of the College.

Dr. Ellesley, meanwhile, was discussing classics, and divinity, and German theology with
the Professors at Geneva, strolling out sometimes alone among the valleys or over the hill-
sides, thinking of Meta, picturing to himself
how pleasant it would be to come home at
the beginning of September and meet her
again, just as he had come to meet Agnes
twenty years ago, after he had been for
that Continental tour with the head-master
of the Millsmany school.

For there was no tumult, no unrest, no
delicious, agonizing uncertainty in this love
which had dawned so quietly upon Fergus
Ellesley's heart. It was no deep need of
his to be ever near the woman to whom he
gave it, within hearing of her voice, within
sight of her meek, quiet face. She was in
his heart continually. His thoughts were
folded round her as lily-leaves around the

flower which is slowly gathering up all its white beauty, and will by-and-by burst from its sheath, the pride and glory of the garden. He felt that she belonged to him in a sweet hold which needed no actual presence to make it more precious. He could have waited for many months, he could have waited for years, thus cherishing the thought of her in his heart, having no fear, knowing no anxiety, giving her all he had to give, never doubting that all would be given to him again. It was the joy of loving, and not the meaner joy of being loved which now, as before, fulfilled Fergus Ellesley's life. It was that giving which enriched him so, which made him almost forget that anything needed to be given for it.

His love was no new revelation to him, the dawn of no life wherein all was strange and untried. Rather it was the taking up

again of that which had never died within
him. His love for Agnes Elliot had been
slumbering all these years. The holy memory
of her, receding further and further away,
had yet been to him all he needed. That
she was no longer near him did not kill the
love he bore to her; that no sweet voice,
or look, or touch, or smile of hers could
reach - him any more, did not destroy his
union with the gentle human soul which had
once spoken to him in all these. But now,
in Meta Waldemar, they spoke to him again.
The love which had been cherished by a
memory so long, was cherished once more
by a living, actual presence. The humble,
unaffected ways, the delicate refinement and
truthfulness, the rare purity of soul and
spirit with which Agnes Elliot had charmed
him twenty years ago, and whose memory
had been to him more than any other hope

could be, were all given back to him in Meta Waldemar. And, as ,though all these slow years had never come and gone, he took up with simple thankfulness and un-questioning faith the old familiar life from which they had parted him.

So the summer days passed on, until the leaves began to look hot and dusty, and the little flowers by the roadside withered, no longer able to bear the hot glances of the August sun, and the Millsmany moors grew purple with bloom of heather, and over all the corn-fields there crept the golden brown tinge of coming harvest-time; and for cool-ness and shade and quietness there was no place like the Carriden-Regis wood, where scarce a gleam of sunshine had leave to enter, except just at evening time, when it struck through the beech-tree clearing, and made a trail of gold among the moss and fern.

What wonder, then, if Stephen Garton, wearied with his studying and teaching, came here to rest sometimes in the hot afternoons; or if Miss Hacklebury and Meta deserted Percy Cottage, on which the sun beat down all the long day, and brought books and work to wile an hour away amongst those fallen trees, close by the little stream where broad iris-leaves made a shelter for blue forget-me-nots, and the white feathery tufts of the meadow-sweet? And was it strange if, knowing where they went, Stephen joined them, and found the time pass so quickly, so pleasantly, as he lay there on the moss, with his book of German Rhine-legends, in which the maidens were all like Meta, and the knights bold, and true, and loving, as he meant to be to her?

They were all there together one after-

noon, when Rodney Charnock and his sister
came sauntering past. Belle Charnock knew
Meta slightly, The two girls had met once
or twice at Mrs. Goverly's, and Mrs. Waldemar had thrown them in each other's way as
much as she could, being anxious for Meta
to get out into society. But they had
not drawn together much, and the acquaintance had almost worn itself out. Besides, Belle did not much care for cultivating the friendship of young ladies who had
no grown-up brothers. That sort of thing
was always a nuisance, she said.

Belle was a tall, showy-looking girl, with
a fine figure and a loud voice and a tolerably effective face. There was a mixture in
her, as in her brother, of Carriden-Regis and
Millsmany, their mother having the family,
and their father the wealth, which, united,
had produced in Belle and Rodney a cross

between the hauteur of the aristocracy proper, and the flash of manufacturing plutocracy. Belle had her brother's free-and-easy swing, his jaunty air of assurance and self-sufficiency, his fashionable bearing and manners. Also a little of his fastness, which she thought becoming rather than otherwise, in a young lady like herself, of good figure and effective appearance.

Stephen was reading aloud; Miss Hacklebury knitting with brisk straightforward activity. The weather never made any difference to her; besides, come what might, those Welsh yarn stockings must be finished before Stephen Garton went to Germany, some time next month, if things turned out so that he got the Burton scholarship, which she devoutly hoped he would. Meta was sitting by her aunt's side, gathering the daisies and pulling off leaf after leaf, to see what the last would say, as Stephen told her the German maidens used to do when their lovers were away. The leaves must have told the right story, for there was a flush of happy brightness on her face, which made her look almost beautiful, as Rodney and his sister strolled past.

The two girls gave each other a formal greeting. Miss Hacklebury jerked out a remark or two on the extreme heat of the weather, Rodney nodded carelessly to Stephen Garton, who returned the nod as carelessly, and then the two saunterers proceeded on their way.

"I say, Belle, who is that pretty girl?" asked Rodney, as soon as they were safely out of hearing. "I haven't come across a prettier since I went to College. Does she hang out anywhere here?"

Belle drew up her five feet six of feminine altitude, and looked scornful.

" You may call her pretty if you like, Rodney. For my part I can't endure such milk-and-water loveliness. Not a bit of style or distinction about her. She is a Miss Waldemar, and she 'hangs out,' as you call it, with her step-mamma at Percy Cottage, just by the churchyard."

Rodney shrugged his shoulders.

" How jealous you girls are. You can't bear to hear any one called pretty, except yourselves. And pray who is Miss Waldemar? I never so much as knew that there was a Miss Waldemar. I suppose you were afraid of my getting hooked in if you introduced me. I'm sure there's never been a Miss Waldemar at Carriden-Regis when I've been home from College before. I don't wonder you didn't want me to see her."

"Nothing of the sort, Rodney," and Belle tossed her head until the pheasant at the top of her hat shook again. "You are quite at liberty to get 'hooked in' as soon as you like, for anything I care about it. Miss Waldemar only came home at Easter, so it is not very likely that you could have been introduced to her before. She used to live with her aunt somewhere in the south, a muff of an old lady, I should think, by the way she brought up her niece. However, she died, and the girl is come home to live with her step-mamma."

"Well, I don't care who she is, or where she comes from; she is an uncommonly pretty girl. There isn't a prettier comes to the College chapel, and you know we see a great many there. They come to have a look at the students.

And Rodney stroked that moustache of his, which had now acquired quite a splendid curl.

"Well," he continued, "all I have to say is this, if you don't take me to Percy Cottage, I'll go by myself, for I mean to know her. I like that style of girl, Belle. She's the sort that will let a fellow have a latch-key and come home late at nights, without doing the tragic over it, and all that sort of thing."

"Oh! I daresay," said Belle, carelessly; "I know she struck me as being very amiable and innocent. She isn't in my line, at all."

"No, she isn't, Belle," said Rodney, glancing at his sister, who, with her high-heeled boots and loud style of jacket, and fancy hat, was altogether a different "line" to Meta Waldemar.

"But if you like, Rodd, I'll call with you. Mrs. Waldemar lent me a book which I haven't taken back yet."

"Done," said Rodney; "I should like to see how she looks without that little black velvet tile. Beautiful lot of hair she has. I shouldn't object to being allowed to stroke it now and then. Don't think Stephen Garton would, either. I suppose he's intending to make up to her. It rather looks as if it was going to be a case. Young man reading at lady's feet with upward glances of admiration; young lady modestly unconscious, downcast eyes, cheek suffused with blushes, &c., spare elderly female on guard. Looks like it, doesn't it, Belle?"

"I don't know," said Belle, snappishly. "Those girls always do contrive to get off, somehow. I can't think what the men are thinking about to be so easily caught. I never heard, though, that Miss Waldemar was engaged."

"I don't care whether she is or not. I

mean to go in for it. But, Belle, do you
think they know what he is?"

"They?—who do you mean by they, Rodney?"

"Why, the maternal party, of course, and
the spare elderly female doing propriety. I
thought Mrs. Waldemar prided herself on
being rather grand in the village, dines at
the good houses, and bows to the best
people; has a basket stuffed with cards, and
all that sort of thing, you know. It doesn't
look much like it, though, to allow her
daughter to marry a washerwoman's son.
Somebody ought to let them know. It
isn't proper. Would *you* like him, now, to
make up to you, and then find out that sort
of thing about him?"

Belle looked as if it would not so very
much signify, so long as the conquest was
achieved. However, she only tossed her head

again, and thrust her hands into the pockets of her jacket. Of course nobody of that sort would ever think of making up to *her*.

"Miss Waldemar's affairs are not of the slightest consequence to me, Rodney. If she chooses to marry this Mr. Garton, I don't see what you and I have to do with it. I suppose she is quite old enough to choose for herself, and I think we have wasted our time over her long enough now."

"There, there, old lady," said Rodney, soothingly, "don't go and put yourself into a state about it. There's no need for you to fling up and be spiteful in that way, just because I happened to admire a pretty girl who isn't exactly like yourself."

Miss Belle only replied, with her chin up in the air higher than ever—

"Like me! No, indeed. I should be very sorry to be like Miss Waldemar. I never saw such a dowdy girl in my life, and I wonder at you, Rodney, for having such wretched taste as to see anything in her worth admiring. You needn't think that I shall do the polite to her, as a future sister-in-law, for I don't intend anything of the sort."

Here the conversation ended, and this loving brother and sister pursued the remainder of their walk in silence, Rodney Charnock turning over in his own mind ways and means for putting himself into Stephen Garton's place.

Rodney was an experienced flirt. He could, when he chose, put on an air of respectful gallantry, which made him a supreme favourite with the ladies, and he was far too fond of admiration not to win as

much of it as possible by all those flattering little attentions to which young girls
are generally so susceptible. He had more
than one dainty little pink note in his desk
at college, written in reply to some tender
words of his; and a packet of tiny white
kid gloves, which he had stolen away at
evening-parties from one blushing maiden
after another, and placed near his heart,
vowing to wear them there for ever. The
students used to joke him sometimes about
these trophies of affection, and tell him that
if he won many more of them, and kept
his promise of wearing them, his evening
waistcoats would begin to present the out-
line of a militia-man's chest, swelling out
beyond all anatomical possibility. Then, too,
he had a bowing acquaintance with almost
all the pretty young ladies in Carriden-Regis, and knew the times of the day at

which they might be met on the pleasant
country roads near the college—a knowledge of which he did not scruple to avail
himself when he was tired of getting up
his examination papers for the Burton scholarship.

Of course it was all fun to him. It sup-
plied the excitement which in that quiet
country place could be procured in no other
way. There was a delicious sense of power
in being able to win those bright smiles,
and to call up a blush on beauty's cheek
by some tender, low-spoken word, which
the listener thought had been breathed to
none before. He judged all other girls, as
most young men do, by those of his own
home. He knew well enough that his sister Belle was as ready to receive flatteries
from her gentlemen friends as he was to
give them to the fair ladies whose fingers

used to tremble in his gentle clasp. He knew that she meant no more by her smiles and wiles and fascinations than he did by all his tender speeches and gallant attentions. They were just put on for the time. They served to pass away a few hours, which might otherwise have lingered heavily along, and to give a spice of piquancy and flavour to the else insufferably dull society of a country village.

Besides, this Meta Waldemar was a very engaging girl, simple, guileless, unsuspecting; quite a new thing in young ladies; a refreshing change from the rather noisy specimens of the sex with whom he had been flirting of late. It would be worth something to win a smile from her. That sweet face must look uncommonly pretty when a conscious blush suffused it; those meek eyes uplifted to his with their shy, pure glance, would produce quite a new sensation—one which he should very much like to experience. He should rather enjoy making an impression on Miss Waldemar, as he had made on so many before; and he was not quite sure that, even if the impression was mutual, he should so very much care about it. If he could achieve a conquest too in that direction, he should feel all the more triumphant from the consciousness of having displaced some one else. And that one Stephen Garton.

Charnock was beginning to hate Stephen Garton as much as a weak, frivolous nature possesses the power to hate. He was galled by the calmness' and indifference with which, of late, Garton had received all his little slights and insults. He had not even appeared to know that they were intended as such, still less to resent them by any of those lofty, scornful looks, which even the charity student could put on when he chose. It was all accounted for now, though. He had met with this girl, and fallen in love with her, and been received into the family on some footing or other, as was evidently the case from the sociable manner in which they were all loitering there together in the wood. And that had set him up, made him feel indifferent to the things which used to vex him before. Also, it had made him forgetful of his lowly origin, a thing which Charnock was determined he never should forget, so long as it was in his power to remind him of it. Nor should other people forget it either.

That was the reason, too, why he was working harder than ever for the Burton scholarship. It seemed to be an accepted fact now amongst the professors that he would get it. None of the other students could stand, they said, against the diligence and perseverance which he was putting forth. And likely enough he was to work hard for it. His success in life depended on a lift of that sort. It would be the merest nonsense for him to fall in love with a girl and ask her to marry him, unless some lucky chance like the Burton prize gave him a start in life. Without it, he might have to wait for years before he could expect to scratch together, by his own unaided exertions, such a home as a respectable girl would care to go to. If indeed any respectable girl would care to go to a home which had been scratched together for her by a washerwoman's son.

Mrs. Waldemar ought to know about Garton's mother, and Mrs. Waldemar *should* know. The young man had most likely got himself in there under false pretences. Dr. Ellesley had a sort of fancy for him, having been the means of bringing him to the College, and had perhaps introduced him to some teaching in the village, and that again had brought him into connection with the Percy Cottage people, who were old residents in the place; at least, Mrs. Waldemar was an old resident, and knew almost everyone.

Of course Dr. Ellelsey would never tell anyone all he knew about him. A due regard for the respectability of the College would prevent that, and Garton himself would be wise enough to keep dark about it. And after all, there was something about him at times which might almost make anybody think that he did not belong to the common sort. So long as no one made inquiries about him, he would pass off very well as a species of genius, one of those eccentric luminaries who have a soul above fancy ties, and can afford, on the strength of their superior intellectual abilities, to go about in thread-bare coats, and seedy wristbands. His want of polish would pass for what some people were fond of calling manliness; his quiet demeanour, and slowness of speech, for the reserve of superior wisdom. There was nothing easier than for a clever man, and Garton certainly was clever, to cover his deficiencies of birth and breeding in this way; and even, if he was only deep enough, to get them imputed to him for excellencies.

Women were unaccountably deceived sometimes by reserve and awkwardness and want of polish in a man. It went up wonderfully with them. Most likely because it was a contrast to their own prettiness and refinement. It made them feel their own superiority, more than they could be expected to feel it in the company of a man of the world like himself, a man up to all the little graces and elegancies of life, and able to meet them on their own ground, so far as politeness and accomplishments went.

But Rodney thought he could put a stop to all that sort of thing. At any rate, he would try. Not so much that he might win Meta Waldemar for himself, as that he might keep Stephen Garton from winning her.

CHAPTER XI.

TOWARDS the beginning of September, about a fortnight after that encounter in the Carriden-Regis wood, Mrs. Waldemar came home for her autumn campaign of planning and contriving.

She knew well that nothing could be gained whilst Dr. Ellesley was away, neither could anything be lost by her own absence from the scene of action. Now, however, that the professors were gathering together again from their various Rhine excursions, boating expeditions, Highland rustications and the like, it behoved her to re-consider her tactics, and rally her forces, and prepare for active service.

Accordingly, to the ill-concealed disappointment of Buttons and Joanna, who had had a glorious summer in their mistress's absence, a letter arrived, announcing that her return might be looked for during the following week. Percy Cottage was scoured from attic to cellar ; carpets renovated, clean curtains put up, every vestige of summer dust removed, the fancy baskets outside the drawing-room and dining-room windows repainted and filled with fresh flowers ; and, a day or two after everything had thus been put into apple-pie-order, Mrs. Waldemar herself, almost lost in trunks and bandboxes, made her appearance.

"So *delighted* to see you, Dorothy Ann, dear," she murmured, as, having been duly welcomed by Miss Hacklebury and Meta at the front door, she glided into the dining-room with swan-like elegance, and sank into the nearest easy-chair, leaving Buttons to see to the disposal of the luggage. "And you too, Meta, my pet, looking so charming. I really never *saw* you look better in my life. Poor dear Mr. Waldemar used always to say, you know, that anybody might have taken us for sisters. And, oh! such a delightful visit as I have had, and *everyone* paying me such attention. I told them it would really quite *spoil* me for home life. Of course, you know, I can't expect such attentions at home, can I, Dorothy Ann?"

"No; I don't suppose you can," replied Dorothy Ann, who felt the old spirit of ineffectual resistance and vexation stirring within her, as sister Waldemar fell into the customary track of self-condolence. "People generally make more fuss over visitors than they do over their own people."

"Yes, but I don't complain, Dorothy Ann,

dear, for I believe you can't help it. You know it was never in your way to pay those delicate little attentions, which I must say are so grateful to me. But so very kind as all dear Mr. Waldemar's friends were; especially his poor uncle, who *would* make me tell him all about the last illness, and dying moments, which upset me so dreadfully, but of course, you know, dear old man, I was obliged to humour him. And oh! such beautiful presents as he made me— immensely wealthy, Dorothy Ann, dear, you know, and if only his poor nephew *had* lived a few years longer, it would have made such a difference to me. Meta, darling, my salts. I feel as if I was going to have an attack. Yes, child, in my satchel on the lobby table."

Meta went in quest of the salts.

"*Such* a difference, for of course at his

age he can't be expected to last much longer, and there would have been no one for it but poor dear Mr. Waldemar. I declare it makes me quite ill to think of it. Thank you, yes, I *should* like the window opened, just a little, a very little. I bore the journey tolerably well, the gentleman who sat opposite was so *very* attentive; really I never travelled with anyone so alive to my wants. But I suppose it is the hot weather oppresses me, or the closeness of the room; you know I am upset directly it—no, no, I *do* believe it is paint. Dorothy Ann, *is* it paint? *Don't* tell me now, that you were so *cruel* as to have paint about, when you *knew* I was coming home, and my nerves are unstrung in a *moment* if I inhale the slightest breath of anything of the kind. Oh, Dorothy Ann! how *could* you?"

And here Mrs. Waldemar would certainly

have given way, had not Meta arrived with the salts, and after a few explosive sobs, equanimity was restored, sister Dorothy Ann looking on meanwhile with a somewhat aggrieved expression of countenance, assuring her sister that nothing in the world had been done but a single coat of paint to the flower-baskets outside the window, and that, as she imagined, by Mrs. Waldemar's own express desire, when she wrote to request the premises to be put in thorough repair before she came home.

"Yes, Dorothy Ann, dear, I daresay it is all right," said Mrs. Waldemar, in the tone of an injured but innocent person. "I've no doubt you did it for the best, and perhaps I *am* very weak and foolish. I know you always thought so, but we won't say anything more about it, only after I have been so *very* much made of all the time I

have been away from home, and such attention paid to me by everyone, and never
allowed to do a *thing* for myself, I *did*
think it was rather hard for me to come
back and none of you to seem moved about
it, and not to offer to take my shawl, or
help me off with my things. It was so very
unlike what I was used to in poor dear Mr.
Waldemar's time."

And Mrs. Waldemar began to sob again,
and sister Dorothy Ann went instinctively
to the cupboard where the sal-volatile was
kept. She had bought a fresh supply only
the day before, thinking sister Waldemar
might very possibly be overset with her
journey, and have an attack.

Buttons, who had heard the preliminary
manifestations, came in to see what was the
matter, inventing an excuse about the boxes.
Being greeted on her entrance by the familiar

odour of the salts, and seeing Meta and Miss Hacklebury standing over the easy-chair, she returned to Joanna with a grunt of disapproval.

"She's on with her nerves again. I wish she'd tie 'em up in a bundle and throw 'em out of the window. I can't abear folks as is always agate over their nerves."

The following Sunday, Mrs. Waldemar, looking more charming than ever in a new costume of suitably mitigated mourning, made her appearance at church, and during the week received, from such of the Carriden-Regis people as were qualified to offer them, their congratulations upon her safe return home after such a protracted absence.

Dr. Ellesley was not amongst the callers. A fact which slightly disconcerted Mrs. Waldemar, until she recollected that, not having

yet attended the College Chapel, the Governor might not be aware of her return. And
then, if he *had* heard of it, being so painfully
shy and retiring, poor dear man! he might
naturally desire to reserve his congratulations
until they could be given more quietly; if,
indeed, he had no other reason for wishing
his visit to be of a private nature. Really,
when Mrs. Waldemar came to think about
it, she was rather pleased than otherwise
that the Doctor should defer his call until
after her more ceremonious acquaintances
had paid theirs. It was rather a compliment than otherwise, for it showed a desire
to place himself upon a different footing than
mere courtesy could give.

But if the Doctor did not call, Miss Belle
Charnock and her brother did, and made
themselves so very agreeable—at least, Mr.
Rodney made himself so very agreeable—that

Mrs. Waldemar, who had never allowed the acquaintance entirely to drop, proposed their coming to spend an evening at Percy Cottage before long. She felt quite convinced, from Mr. Rodney's exceeding impressiveness and urbanity towards Meta, that he had his own private reasons for making this call, and she was quite disposed, from what she knew of his position and prospects, to give him every facility in pursuing the acquaintance.

The invitation was given with easy familiarity, and only to Miss Charnock.

"Just a quiet evening amongst ourselves, Miss Charnock. I am so anxious for you and Meta to know each other. In fact, I have set my mind upon it ever since she came home; but, you see, having been away nearly the whole of the summer, I have not been able to see so much of my friends as

I could wish. However, *now* I hope you will come and see us very often. *Do* say, now, that you will come and see us very often. And pray bring your work and your music with you on Thursday evening, and let us have a dear, quiet, cosy little time. You don't know how I enjoy a real cosy evening. It is so *much* pleasanter than indiscriminate society, *is* it not, dear Miss Charnock?"

Miss Charnock did not think it was. She rather liked indiscriminate society, but she could not be so rude as to say so in the face of Mrs. Waldemar's undisguised preference for the sweetness of more private friendship. She accepted the invitation, rather as if she were conferring a favour than receiving one.

"And if Mr. Charnock *would* do us the favour," suggested Mrs. Waldemar, as though it were quite an after-thought. "And if you would *like* to step in after tea, you know we should be so delighted to see you. I really feel that I ought not to press it upon you, because we have no gentlemen at Percy Cottage, and I am so afraid you might feel it dull; but still, you know, if you would *like* to join us in a little music during the evening."

Whereupon Mr. Rodney said something almost impassioned about the extreme delight it would give him to spend an evening at Percy Cottage. And he assured Mrs. Waldemar, garnishing the assurance with sundry of those polite compliments which he knew so well how to intersperse when occasion served, that he had been longing for an introduction ever since he returned from college in June; only circumstances hitherto had been unfavourable, Mrs. Waldemar having been so much from home. But he could not tell her how glad he should be to avail himself of her kindness, and how refreshing a little really refined feminine society always appeared to him after being shut up for a whole term-time with nothing but noisy students, some of them anything but gentlemanly.

Mr. Charnock put that last sentence very expressively, hoping that Mrs. Waldemar might be induced by his manner to make more minute inquiries as to the individuals implicated in the charge of ungentlemanliness. However, she did not take it in that light, and after arranging that he should accompany his sister Belle on Thursday, she allowed her visitors to depart, purposing in her own mind to cultivate their acquaintance with all possible assiduity, until she saw how things were likely to turn out with respect to Stephen Garton.

Because that affair about the Burton scholarship was quite undecided as yet, and if by any chance Mr. Garton should not be the successful competitor, she could never be guilty of such imprudence as to allow anything like an attachment to spring up between him and Meta. These long engagements, as she had said before, were such dreadful nuisances. Meta might be hanging on for years, waiting until Mr. Garton got into something, thereby proving a most serious hindrance to her own chances of success. Indeed, until the girl was suitably settled for life, it was next to impossible for her to achieve anything like a desirable position for herself; and therefore she should never think of encouraging the young man unless this scholarship fell to his lot, and so made an early marriage both practicable and advisable for him.

And for that reason, too, the uncertainty of young Garton's prospects, and of Meta's as involved in them, she must take her step-daughter out as much as possible into society, so as to rub off a little of that nonsensical shyness which made her ready to put herself anywhere out of sight if a visitor came near the house. Such ridiculous folly in a girl of twenty! Why, when *she* was that age, she knew as much of the world as Meta would know when she was fifty, and a great deal more too, and could contrive for herself in it, and arrange for her own interests, as Meta never seemed to have the slightest notion of doing.

However, if the girl could not look after her own interests, somebody else must look after them for her. Mr. Charnock was very gentlemanly and agreeable, and evidently quite bent upon forming an intimacy. And his success in life, too, did not depend, like Mr. Garton's, on the winning of that scholarship. The Charnocks were very wealthy people. The young man had only been studying for the last year or two at the new college until his uncle, one of the most important merchants in Millsmany, was ready to take him into his office, and then into partnership, when he would at once step into a splendid position, and be able to settle whenever he chose.

How very fortunate, under the circumstances, then, that she had made up her mind to prudence in that affair of Mr. Garton's. If she had encouraged him to come to the point, as he no doubt was disposed to do from the very beginning of their acquaintance, and allowed Meta to become entangled with him to the exclusion of an opportunity so much more eligible as this which had now turned up, she should never have been able to forgive herself for such a piece of blundering. The girl's prospects might have been ruined for life, and her own most seriously marred. As things were now, however, that intimacy with young Garton, which perhaps had been allowed to go a *little* too far, might be dropped without any ill-natured comment from people disposed to gossip about such matters. The College duties were just beginning, which would of course prevent him from coming into the village so frequently. And then in the event of his getting the Burton prize, which, after all, would not place him in nearly so good a position as that which Rodney Charnock occupied at present, he would be disposed of at once, go to Germany most likely; and then, by the time he returned, things would be so far arranged for Meta's settlement, that anything like a renewal of his former intimacy at Percy Cottage would be out of the question.

So Mrs. Waldemar thought within herself, as she watched Belle Charnock and her brother sauntering leisurely down the Carriden-Regis road, after their morning call.

CHAPTER XII.

MEANWHILE Meta, unconscious Meta, for whose benefit—subordinate of course to that of her elegant step-mamma—all this planning and counter-planning had been carried on, was drifting nearer and nearer to that golden shore of hope and promise, from which, once reached, there is no return any more to the colder, yet oft-times safer haven whence the voyager set forth.

Miss Hacklebury was quite correct in those suspicions which, nevertheless, she hid so wisely in her own faithful heart. With a mingling of maidenly pride and reserve, Meta had fought at first with that ever-strengthening hold which Stephen Garton's more powerful nature was gaining upon her own. She tried to make herself believe that she did not care for him; that it was no consequence to her whether he came to Percy Cottage or not; that she could be just as happy, just as contented, without him; and that it would not make a bit of difference if he went away and never spoke to her any more at all. That was when Miss Hacklebury noticed the touch of saucy independence in her hitherto quiet, gentle little niece. Then the hold became stronger. It was no use any longer to chide herself for the sweet thoughts of him which kept stealing into her heart. The days were only bright now as Stephen Garton brightened them. There was no peace for her, no quietness, no joy, save as he brought it. And when he did not come, the days

seemed so weary. Or if, coming, he chanced
to speak not so kindly, a thought, the
thought that he did not care for her, made
a sudden darkness all around. And yet, why
should he care? That was when Miss Hacklebury saw the restless look on Meta's face,
chasing its happy content away, as passing
summer clouds chase the sunshine from ripen-
ing harvest fields. Then, little by little, she
learned to trust him. Some gentle look,
some loving word brought the sunshine back
again. Some sweet breeze of hope lifted
the mists from that golden shore whither
she was voyaging, and showed her how
bright it was, how little she needed, nearing it day by day, to long for the quiet
haven she had left behind. That was when
Miss Hacklebury saw the light begin to
deepen in Meta's eyes, and the happy smile
to quiver on her face; and learned from

these things that the girl had passed, whether for joy or sorrow she knew not, the calm, unquestioning content of her young life.

And now surprise, resistance, fear, were all passed. Stephen and Meta knew that they loved each other. How they found it out was of no consequence. To Meta, innocent, unworldly little maiden that she was, it made not one bit of difference that Stephen had never conveyed to her the important fact of his love in a set speech. She had never thought about that at all. She just loved him with her whole heart. All she had to give she gave to him. That, before she was quite sure that he loved her in return, was a distress and a grief to her. It filled her with such a tumult and unrest as she had never felt before. She fancied she had done something wrong. She could not bear to look Stephen Garton in the face.

She dreaded for him to come to the house, and yet if he did not come, his absence was a pain far worse than the dread. Now all that had passed away. The changing, restless, rainbow tints of hope, fear, uncertainty, longing, had blended into the white splendour of happy love. She feared no more then; there seemed scarcely anything even to hope for, for her life came to be just one long thought of him; and giving all, she knew, though how she could not tell, that all was given to her again.

That was the little maiden whose favour Rodney Charnock set himself to win when he and his sister Belle went to pay their promised visit to Percy Cottage one pleasant Thursday evening early in September; Belle assuring him beforehand that there was nothing she disliked so much as these quiet opportunities, and that he must not expect her, after this preliminary courtesy had been disposed of, to be any further assistance to him in cultivating the acquaintance of his new flame.

Rodney had sufficient confidence in his own powers of fascination to inform her that he should not require any assistance. To tell the truth, he began to feel rather interested in the little Waldemar girl, as he called Meta. Perhaps the very unconsciousness with which she received his flatteries, or the pretty shyness with which she seemed to turn away from them when they were so manifest that she could not but understand their meaning, gave him more pleasure in offering them. He felt all the charm of a game at chance now, whereas in his former flirtations he had known the conclusion from the beginning. The skill had all been on his side; and as an experienced chess-player does not so much care to play when he knows he will win, so Rodney Charnock was rather tired of laying siege to hearts which, almost before the first shot was fired, surrendered at discretion. This heart did not seem to surrender at all. It did not even seem to know that it was expected to do so.

Mrs. Waldemar watched his attentions during the evening with bland satisfaction, congratulating herself more than ever upon the admirable prudence which had kept Meta in a position to profit by them. And really, now that young Mr. Charnock had come upon the field, and she contrasted his fascinating manners with the almost boorish awkwardness, as she called it, of Stephen Garton, she wondered that she could ever have allowed herself to look favourably upon anything of that kind for Meta. This connection would be in all respects so much more desirable, besides avoiding months, if not years, of suspense and uncertainty with regard to her future position. Because, even if, as she said before, that Burton prize was gained, it was not such a very wonderful thing after all—not nearly so advantageous as a partnership in one of the best Millsmany firms. Why, as the wife of Rodney Charnock, Meta might have a handsome villa residence in Carriden-Regis, and keep her carriage, and mix with the very best society of the place, who, in consideration of her late poor dear papa's position, and Mrs. Charnock's own connections, would look upon her as completely different to the generality of the wealthy manufacturing people of the neighbourhood. Whereas, if she waited for Stephen Garton, there was no telling what sort of a home he might be able to take her to, or what sort of a position he might give her; he being a man never likely to make much figure in society, and Meta being a girl who would never push her own way into anything better than what her husband could command. How very fortunately things had turned out!

But Mrs. Waldemar felt that she must not allow such reflections as these, though pleasing in the extreme, to interfere with the flow of hospitable attention towards the guest who had been the means of causing them to take root and flourish in her mind. Mr. Charnock had looked in, according to promise, after tea, and was now chatting away with Meta in the bay window, professing to be lost in admiration of the very unpretending little scrap of fancy-work with which she was beguiling the time.

"You know, Mr. Charnock," the solicitor's widow remarked, blandly regarding the young people from the couch on which she was reclining with such graceful negligence, " I thought after you were gone the other day, that I had been so *very* selfish to persuade you to look in upon us this evening, knowing that we should have no gentlemen to meet you. I always fancy gentlemen are so *very* dull alone, and you know I should be so distressed to think you were not enjoying yourself. Miss Charnock, now, I appeal to *you*,. what shall we do to keep your brother from feeling dull? Is there anything in the *world* we can do to amuse him?"

Belle, who was secretly voting the evening a nuisance, she had no love for petticoat gatherings, as she called them, suppressed a yawn, and replied,

"Oh! Rodney looks after himself, I assure you. I never think of such a thing as trying to amuse him. He can always manage well enough, if only he has plenty of ladies to chatter to. I do believe, after being shut up amongst all those young men at the College so long, he almost hates the sight of a coat. Pray don't distress yourself about him. He will do very well."

"Oh, dear! yes. I had quite forgotten that," exclaimed Mrs. Waldemar, with a sudden gush of enthusiasm. "Of *course* you are one of Dr. Ellesley's students; and did I not hear, yes, I am *sure* I am not mistaken, Meta, darling, did not young Garton tell us that Mr. Charnock was one of the competitors for the Burton prize?"

"The successful one, I hope, too," continued Mrs. Waldemar, with an expressive smile. "Meta, my pet, I'm sure you hope, don't you now, that Mr. Charnock will be the successful competitor?"

Meta only blushed, which might mean anything. She did not say whether or not she was very anxious for Mr. Charnock to win the prize. But Mrs. Waldemar's words, as Rodney thought, certainly implied that she was not very anxious for Mr. Garton to get it. And yet, if things had been as he thought they were, if Stephen Garton was looking forward to entering the Percy Cottage family as a son-in-law, Mrs. Waldemar ought to be anxious that he should gain the prize. At least, it was rather a strange thing for her to express a hope that anyone else should get it.

Unless,—and Rodney caressed that moustache of his. Such a state of things as his vanity suggested certainly was by no means improbable. He was an eligible young man, a very eligible young man. He had been told that fact so often, by words and looks, and

g, he almost hates the

don't distress yourself

be very well."

I had quite forgotten

n. Waldemar, with a

nism. "Of course you

's students; and did I

I am not mistaken,

young Garton tell us

the competi-

r

too," continu-

expressive smi

you hope

will be

Meta only blushed, which might mean anything. She did not say whether or not she was very anxious for Mr. Charnock to win the prize. But Mrs. Waldemar's words, as Rodney thought, certainly implied that she was not very anxious for Mr. Garton to get it. And yet, if things had been as he thought they were, if Stephen Garton was looking forward to entering the Percy Cottage family as a son-in-law, Mrs. Waldemar ought to be anxious that he should gain the prize. At least, it was rather a strange **thing for** her to express a hope that anyone else should get it.

Unless,—and Rodney caressed t'

blushes and various other little insinuations, that really he was beginning to feel as if he did not care to hear it any more. It was quite possible that Mrs. Waldemar might think on the whole, &c., &c., Rodney took in the state of the case at a glance.

" Thank you, Mrs. Waldemar," he replied with an air of supreme indifference, " I—it does not signify very much to me. I just put my name on the list as I had not much studying to do, and I have no doubt if I tried I should be able to carry it off. But you see the honour is not worth much to me, as I am not looking forward to professional life; and as for the little temporary stipend connected with it, many of the other students need that much more than I do."

"Oh! yes," Mrs. Waldemar said, "we all know that you would never think anything of the mere pecuniary results. Those, of course, are *quite* below your consideration. But then you know, Mr. Charnock, honour is such a *delightful* thing. Oh! I do think if I were a man, I should have such a *passion* for honour."

Rodney smiled, as he always did when ladies went into their little enthusiasms about honour and all that sort of nonsense.

"Yes, the honour is all very well, and really sometimes I feel almost sorry I have not gone in for it with more determination, though it would be the easiest thing in the world for me to get it, even yet. But, indeed, to tell you the truth, Mrs. Waldemar, I should scarcely feel justified in taking it over the head of such a fellow as Garton. It wouldn't be giving him a fair chance, you know."

Here was a fine opportunity for Rodney

to bring out what he wished his elegant
hostess to know about the poor divinity
student. And to bring it out, too, in the
setting of his own noble disinterestedness,
so winning praise for himself, whilst appear-
ing to give it to another. Accordingly he
altered his tone from easy indifference to
the grave deliberateness of a man who has
made up his mind to some lofty act of self-
denial.

"It wouldn't be giving him a fair chance,
you know, Mrs. Waldemar; and, of course,
to a poor fellow in his position, it is of all
the consequence in the world whether he
gets a lift like that. I should positively
despise myself if I took a prize from him,
and that poor mother of his starving herself as she does to scrape together a few
shillings for him, in order that he may not
have to borrow from the Governor."

"Oh! Mr. Charnock," and Mrs. Waldemar clasped her hands in a second demonstration of feminine enthusiasm, "how *noble* of you, how splendidly unselfish! Meta, my darling, did you *ever* hear of anything so splendidly unselfish? Oh! Miss Charnock, how proud you must feel of your brother, to think that he is capable of making such a sacrifice. The very *idea* of giving up the Burton scholarship for the sake of letting a poorer student take it! Oh! I *do* call that so noble! I can't *tell* you how noble I call it!"

Mr. Rodney deprecated the praise. It was really more than he could think of appropriating.

"Oh! no, no, Mrs. Waldemar. It is nothing at all, nothing at all. You know we fellows at College always make up our minds to do that sort of thing for each

other. We never come down hard upon anyone like Garton when there is a little money
in the case. You know, poor wretch, a little
money is everything to him."

"Ah! that is very beautiful of you, Mr.
Charnock," said Mrs. Waldemar, the enthusiasm gathering force as it proceeded.
"You know you only add fresh honour to
your disinterestedness by attempting to conceal it. Of course we *all* know how *very*
easily you could have carried off the prize,
and I *do* think it is so splendid of you to
let anyone else take it. Really, Mr. Charnock, you make me feel quite *excited* to
think about it. Poor dear Mr. Waldemar
used to say there was nothing roused me
so much as to hear of a deed of lofty self-
denial; you don't know how it stirs me up.
But tell me, Mr. Charnock, would it *really*
be such an object to him, poor Garton I

mean, you know? Is he *really* so very dependent on anything of that sort? I always understood that his connections were not first-class, but still, you know, a young man of talent may get over an obstacle of that kind, if there is nothing absolutely disgraceful."

Rodney dismissed that subject with a wave of the hand, which spoke volumes for the absolute disgracefulness of Stephen Garton's antecedents.

"Excuse me, Mrs. Waldemar. It was very imprudent of me to mention such a delicate subject, but I assure you I was under the impression that everything had been confided to you, or I would not for one moment have injured the young man's prospects by alluding to anything so—so——in fact, I would rather not say any more about it. I feel that I have transgressed already."

"Oh! Mr. Charnock!" gasped Mrs. Waldemar, the enthusiasm suddenly collapsing into agonizing suspense, "is it anything *dreadful?* *Do* tell me. And to think that I should have introduced him to Mrs. Goverly, one of the best people in the village. *Don't* say it is anything disgraceful, Mr. Charnock, or I am sure I shall never be able to bear it."

"Rodney," said Belle in her loud noisy tones, "you are enough to frighten one into fits. Why can't you tell Mrs. Waldemar and have done with it, instead of making such a mystery about it? Mr. Garton's mother is a washerwoman, Mrs. Waldemar; that is all— takes in clear starching and laces and such things, and lives in a little back street somewhere in Millsmany; excellent old soul, I believe, and had a great deal to bear with her husband, who was drunken and scampish, and that style of thing."

Mrs. Waldemar began to have the preliminary symptoms of an attack.

"Meta, my salts—quick! Oh! if Dorothy Ann was here to give me my sal-volatile. A—a—oh, dear! I really cannot bring myself to speak the odious word. A *laundress* did you say, Miss Charnock? Is it possible —a laundress? Oh! tell me that I did not understand you correctly. And to think— Meta, *do* get the salts out of my work-table quickly, I believe I shall give way, it is so very dreadful; and to think that I should have allowed him to come in and out of the house like one of ourselves. Dear me! such a shock. *Do* excuse me; but you know poor dear Mr. Waldemar used to have to be so careful of me—never allowed anything of this kind to be mentioned to me suddenly, for fear it might bring on spasms, though of course you could not be expected to understand my nervous system, so painfully sensitive."

And Mrs. Waldemar sobbed explosively.

"Rodney," said Belle, "Mrs. Waldemar is going into hysterics. Can't you hold the salts for her. What a stupid you are to raise such a commotion about nothing."

Rodney was up in an instant, bending over the prostrate lady with a tender solicitude which the late poor dear Mr. Waldemar, in his most sympathetic moods, could scarcely have surpassed.

"*Dear* Mrs. Waldemar, a *thousand* pardons. I am so distressed. I really never intended, do let me assure you I never intended——"

"Oh! don't apologize," gasped Mrs. Waldemar, with a spasmodic attempt at a smile. "It was very foolish of me, I *know* it was. Another time, you know, you will understand me better; a sudden shock always has this effect upon me: such frightful sensitiveness, is it not? And yet, you know, I ought to be so *very* much obliged to you for breaking it to me, if I could only—Meta, darling, run upstairs for my vinaigrette, it revives me so beautifully after an attack of this kind, if I could *only* get over the shock. And to think, you know, that dear Mrs. Ellesley never told me. Only hinted about struggling with difficulties, and his connections not being able to do much for him. Thank you, Mr. Charnock, you are so very kind, I *do* think I can sit up now."

Rodney withdrew his supporting arm. He wished Meta instead of Mrs. Waldemar had had the attack.

"Mrs. Ellesley certainly ought to have prepared you for something of the kind," he said with suitable gravity. "Only, you know, the Governor don't like it talked about. It might do the college harm if anything of the kind got abroad. And we all of us respect the old fogie—I mean we all of us have such a regard for Dr. Elles-ley, that we should never for a moment think of distressing him by naming anything of the kind. And so long as Garton kept within bounds, of course there was no need to make a stir about it. But when he en-deavours to thrust himself, as I may say, into the friendship of a family like yours, Mrs. Waldemar, it becomes the duty of a gentleman——"

"Oh! yes, yes, Mr. Charnock, and I *do* assure you I feel so very *much* obliged to you for naming it. And so kind as we have been to him, too. It is really fright-ful to think about it. Oh! thank you, Meta, darling, you have brought my vinaigrette, and now if you would *just* fetch me a glass of water. Meta has such wonderful nerve, Mr. Charnock; or I think I ought to say she has no nerves at all. You see this terrible affair does not appear to make the slightest impression upon her. There is such a difference in people. Poor dear Mr. Waldemar used to say I was nothing but a bundle of nerves, and I do believe he was right."

Meta set off for the water. She had heard all about Stephen's mother, long ago. He had told her himself, not many days after he began to teach at the Goverlies. He would have told Mrs. Waldemar, too, before he accepted her invitation to make himself at home at Percy Cottage, only she had said to him so very emphatically,

"Mrs. Ellesley has told us *all* about you, Mr. Garton. I assure you we have heard *all* about you, and I do feel *so* interested. I do so *dote* upon talent that has risen from the ranks."

That was enough for Stephen's honest self-respect. He did not feel that any further information was due to Mrs. Waldemar after that. But he could not rest until Meta knew from himself who and what he was; all the history of those early struggles, and the long years of toil which that patient self-denying old mother had borne for him, before he could even stand where most young men stand without any labour or trouble of their own, at a good starting-point in the race for success.

Meta listened, and thought him more of a hero than ever. That he was less worthy to be loved because poverty and hardship had written their story on his youth, was a thought that never crossed her innocent

heart. Nay, as she listened with shy, wondering delight to the history of his life,
there mingled with her love for him a
new reverence and pride; and, but that she
never dared to speak of him to any one,
she thought how pleasant it would be to
tell Aunt Hacklebury all about him, to let
her know what a hero this Stephen Garton was, this man who had struggled up
so far and thrust out of his way barrier
after barrier, until now he could stand,
proudly level in learning and worth, with
any man in the world.

So Meta listened quietly enough to all
that Mr. Charnock had to say. She did
not think it would ever make any difference to her. And as her mamma so often
had attacks about things which passed over
and were never mentioned any more, it was
likely enough that this little bit of village

gossip, which at the time of its telling had produced such a wondrous commotion, would by-and-by sink quietly into the same oblivion.

CHAPTER XIII.

MRS. WALDEMAR'S tactics, so far as Meta's prospective settlement was involved in them, were progressing triumphantly. She had every reason to be abundantly satisfied with the manner in which Mr. Charnock had availed himself of the facilities placed at his disposal, and she fully believed that Meta had only to conduct herself wisely, and in the course of a few months, or a year at most—for Mr. Charnock was going into his uncle's office soon after Christmas—take her place as an envied and successful married woman amongst the best families of the place.

Her own plans were not succeeding quite so well. The Doctor did not call, and he had now been at home a fortnight. Which piece of inattention, as she could not help considering it, began to annoy Mrs. Waldemar not a little, the more so as it was impossible for her to open fire in the direction of the College, until a preliminary salute had been given from the garrison there.

Still, as she said to herself, there were so many things to be attended to at the opening of the session, especially as this examination was coming on in the course of a day or two. Indeed, Mr. Charnock, who had very politely called upon her the day after his visit, to inquire if the effects of her attack had quite passed away, said that some of the Professors from distant Colleges, who were to take part in the proceedings, had already arrived, and were staying with the Governor. Of course, as Mrs. Ellesley was too far advanced in years to do very much towards the entertaining of guests, especially learned men like the Professors, Dr. Ellesley's time would be very much taken up, and possibly he was intending to put off his call at Percy Cottage until he could come in some day towards the close of the afternoon, and join them in a quiet cup of tea. That would be so much better than a formal visit. Doubtless as soon as the examination was over, and the strange Professors had gone away, she might expect him to drop in and spend a few hours with them.

In which expectation she was confirmed by Meta, who, coming in from a walk a few days after Belle Charnock's visit, said,

"Mamma, where do you think I have been?"

"I don't know, my dear," said Mrs. Waldemar, captiously. "How am I to tell where you go when you never ask me to go with you?"

And she said no more than that, for she was beginning to be tired of this long armistice between the College and the Cottage.

"I have been to see Mrs. Ellesley, mamma. We have been walking about in the grounds nearly all the morning. They look so beautiful now."

There was animation enough in Mrs. Waldemar's tones, as she replied to this remark, but it was the animation of asperity.

"Meta, how *could* you think of such a thing as going there to make a call without me to chaperone you? I am surprised at you; it is positively indecorous. And amongst all those young men, too!"

"I did not see any of the young men,

mamma. I did not know there was any-thing wrong in it."

"I did not say there was anything wrong in it; but your own good sense ought to tell you that it is a very improper thing for a young girl like you to go out making calls alone, and upon a lady of Mrs. Elles-ley's standing. When you choose to make visits again without me, confine them to girls of your own age."

"I thought you would be glad to know that I had gone, mamma," said Meta, simply. "You told Mrs. Ellesley you should be glad for me to go out by myself a little more, be-cause I was too shy."

"Meta, don't stand there arguing with me in that manner. I *insist* upon it that from this day you never go to the ·College again without my permission. Do you understand me?"

"Yes, mamma. I saw Dr. Ellesley, too, and he sent a message for you."

Mrs. Waldemar's accents softened. So did the expression of her face.

"Indeed, my love. Pray what did he say?"

"He said he was very sorry he had not been able to call at Percy Cottage since you came home, but the preparations for the examination have taken up all his time."

"How *exceedingly* kind of him! I must say I had wondered a little that we had not seen him. And I hope, Meta, my love, you told him we should be delighted to have a call from him?"

"I did not say we should be delighted. I told him we should be very glad if he liked to come. And he asked how long it was since you had returned."

Mrs. Waldemar smiled and simpered.

"Indeed, my love. I do not know what consequence that could be to him. But perhaps, as I have not been to the College Chapel since I came home, he might think I was still away. Anything else, my pet?"

"Yes, mamma, he said he would come as soon as the examination was over, and perhaps take a cup of tea with us."

"Very well, darling," said Mrs. Waldemar, quietly, but there was a flush of triumph upon her dark cheek. "And has my pet anything else to tell me?"

"No, mamma, I think not. Oh! I met Mr. Charnock as I was coming home."

"Did you? Well, I daresay, shy little creature that you are, you ran away from him. Come now, my sweet, confess to me. *Did* you run away from him?"

"No, mamma," said Meta, with almost

quaint simplicity. She never could return any of Mrs. Waldemar's affectionate expletives, either in public, or when, on such rare occasions as the present, they were bestowed in the familiar intercourse of private life. "He turned and came nearly all the way home with me, and he asked me if he might bring me some new music to practise."

"And you told him he might. You know, darling, I am so anxious for you to improve your voice. You could sing so prettily, my pet, if only you had some one to practise with."

"No, mamma, I told him I couldn't sing; but he said he would come and sing them to me, so it was no consequence."

"You are a little goose. I don't know when I shall make a woman of you. But run away and take your hat off. You have quite a pretty colour, I declare, when you come in out of the fresh air. And, stay, take this note to Buttons, and tell her to leave it at Mrs. Goverly's when she goes for the bread to-night. What days does Mr. Garton go there?"

"Wednesdays, mamma; but he does not have to go at all now, for the children are away at the seaside. It is fortunate for him, because it leaves him more time for his examination. Mamma, do you really wish that Mr. Charnock would get the prize? I thought you told Mr. Garton you should be so delighted for him to be successful."

"Run away, darling. I have a headache coming on. And don't forget the note for Buttons, to be left this evening."

Meta disappeared, leaving her mamma to a second meditation, which, judging from the expression it produced on Mrs. Waldemar's countenance, was decidedly more agreeable than that which her step-daughter's return had interrupted.

For she really had begun to think, before Meta came in from her morning walk, that the citadel against which she had been directing her artillery had capitulated to another invader. Dr. Ellesley might have met with some one during his Continental travels, in whose hands he had placed the keys of that garrison whose surrender she, Mrs. Waldemar, had counted upon as almost certain. Men at his time of life did sometimes commit themselves in that way; men as grave and retiring, and apparently unlikely for anything of the sort as the Governor of Carriden-Regis College. And really in that case she thought she should never have been able to get over her mortification and vexation. She did not think she

could ever have stayed in the neighbourhood comfortably, if any one but herself
had been installed into the governor-general-
ship of that handsome suite of rooms, and
had assumed the dispensing of the College hospitalities, and the sustaining of Dr.
Ellesley's position as head of the concern.

But that message altered everything. It
showed a desire on the Doctor's part to
remove their intimacy still farther from anything like formality, and place it on the
footing of a familiar friendship. The plan
which he proposed was so much more promising for the ultimate success of her own
scheme, than if he had satisfied himself with
leaving his card, like the rest of her friends,
when he knew that she had returned home;
or merely made a state call and gone through
a little formal conversation in the presence of
strangers. He evidently longed for something

private and unrestrained. He preferred these quiet social opportunities when the observances of etiquette could be laid aside, and the communion of kindred minds could be carried on without interruption.

Accordingly, the day after the examination, Mrs. Waldemar attired herself with becoming elegance—since returning from her sojourn with old Mr. Waldemar, she had still further discarded the deeper manifestations of grief, having only continued them throughout that visit from motives of expediency—and took her station with a bit of delicate embroidery in her hand, in the bay-window, an admirable post for an external survey, since it commanded the Millsmany road for nearly a mile, beside affording a side-view of the lane which led down to the upper end of Carriden-Regis wood.

As the September sunlight began to strike

slantingly through the beech-trees on the village green, a tall, stooping figure, clothed in professional black, hove in sight from the little gate which led out of the wood into the high road; and with a start of admirably feigned surprise, Mrs. Waldemar exclaimed,

" Sister Dorothy Ann! I *do* believe that is Dr. Ellesley coming out of the wood. Just you look, now, and tell me if you don't think it is."

Dorothy Ann rose deliberately, and crossed the room to the bay window, thus bringing her prim figure and tasteless costume into what Mrs. Waldemar felt was a most effective contrast to her own surpassing elegance.

Certainly as they stood together, there was a family likeness between the two sisters. Both were tall of stature and spare of figure. Both had the same complexion, the same dark hair and eyes, and the same somewhat distinctive features, though moulded by character into a totally different expression. But sister Hacklebury was like a bit of dry seaweed which had been picked out with a pin into as near an approach to natural arrangement as the circumstances will permit; whereas sister Waldermar was like a specimen from the same pool, which some more experienced marine botanist has flooded with a current of water, so allowing each spray and fibre to take its own graceful fall, and dispose itself at its own sweet will. There was this advantage about sister Hacklebury, however. Such as she was, she would last. The hard, dry bit of seaweed had already lost all that it could lose in the way of beauty, and might safely be depended upon to retain its present appearance for years, not lacking, when looked at through a sufficiently powerful microscope, some little touch of comeliness hidden from the common eye; but sister Waldemar, as soon as that artificial current was discontinued, would shrivel up into useless ugliness, not even good for a barometer to ascertain the change of the atmosphere, for the bath of hard water in which she had been steeped for so many years had effectually destroyed all natural properties which once she might have possessed.

"Yes," said sister Hacklebury, going back to her seat and resuming her work, after having scanned through a pair of gold-rimmed spectacles the tall stooping figure which was gradually emerging into distinctness. "It *is* the Doctor. I could tell him amongst a thousand by that walk of his, so like our poor old clergyman at Poplarcroft. I always said, from the very first, they were alike as two peas, Dr. Ellesley and our dear old Poplarcroft clergyman. It's study makes them stoop so, that's what it is, though it don't seem to take that effect on everybody."

"Then, sister Dorothy Ann," said Mrs. Waldemar, "he is coming here to tea, and we must have the pea-green china down."

But Miss Hacklebury made no reply to that remark, she only stitched away the more vigorously than ever at a capital G, which she was working in red silk on a stout, useful, comfortable-looking Welsh yarn stocking.

"There, then," she said, regarding it, when the letter was finished, with an air of affectionate satisfaction. "That stocking is fit for a prince, and I don't care who says it. And I don't believe there's a prince in the world either, who ever got more kindness knitted into a stocking than I've knitted into that for Stephen Garton. There are only two pairs more to mark now, and the heels to darn, I must have them darned for him because they wear so much longer, and then Buttons shall take them down to the College, with my compliments, and I've sent them for Mr. Garton."

Buttons shall do no such thing, thought Mrs. Waldemar to herself, having decided on quite a different course of action with respect to poor Stephen. But she was not going to tell Miss Hacklebury that, for Miss Hacklebury could put out a wonderful amount of stubbornness when she chose; and, feeling as she did feel towards the young man, she would resist energetically any open attempts to injure him. If you wanted to do anything with Dorothy Ann, you must take her by guile. Besides, Stephen Garton was by no means the most important matter in hand, when every moment Dr. Ellesley was nearing Percy Cottage.

" The stockings look very comfortable, Dorothy Ann. I'm sure it's very good of you to take so much trouble for strangers, though I daresay if you had had the mind to do them for your own relations, you might have found someone nearer home that would have been glad of a set for winter. But that pea-green china must be got down. The Doctor would never have come at this time in the afternoon if he had not meant stopping tea."

" We'll wait and see if he comes," said Dorothy Ann, sententiously, " and then we'll wait and see if he means tea. It strikes me he didn't exactly mean it when he came that other afternoon, only he isn't as ready with his tongue as some people." This was a hit in answer to sister Waldemar's home-thrust about the stockings. "The Doctor isn't a man that means tea in a general way when he goes out. That pea-green china has scarcely had time to get itself rested on the pegs since it was had down for the Charnocks."

"Then it wont want dusting," said sister Waldemar, readily.

"Yes, it will. Do you think I would ever show such a want of respect to poor grand-mother's china as to have it used without dusting it properly? They were almost mo-ther's last words to me before she died, 'Dorothy Ann,' she said, 'you'll take care of that china for my sake and your dear grandmother's?' and I promised her as good as on my bended knees that I would do everything for it that was proper, and I mean to do; and I think, sister Waldemar, you might have more consideration for it yourself than to want it disturbed again."

Sister Waldemar felt in her pocket for her salts and began to sob. There was nothing affected her nerves like contradiction, it broke her down directly, she used to say. But there was no time for a manifestation now, for even whilst Miss Hacklebury was expatiating on the respect due to the pea-green china, Dr. Ellesley had crossed the road and his hand was on the latch of the garden gate. Mrs. Waldemar sprang up with charming impulsiveness, and went out into the lobby to meet him.

"So *glad* to see you, Dr. Ellesley, so *very* glad, and so *kind* of you to come and see us in this delightfully unceremonious way. You know I *do* so like my friends to be unceremonious. And just as we were going to sit down to an early cup of tea, too, so *very* fortunate, for you will join us, Doctor, now, *will* you not? I am sure you cannot be so naughty as to run away from us just when we are going to sit down to tea."

The Doctor allowed himself to be persuaded. Indeed, he had partly come with the intention of staying. It was such a long time since he had seen Meta, except during that chance interview of the day before. And to sit beside her for a little while, and to look into her quiet face, and to hear the tones of her voice again, would be such a pleasant rest after the toil and labour of those examination days. So he promised, and Mrs. Waldemar conducted him triumphantly into the sitting-room, pouring out all the way a torrent of affectionate inquiries.

"And how is dear Mrs. Ellesley? I have been longing so to call and see her ever since I returned from town, but I have been so dreadfully busy—such *oceans* of calls every day, as soon as the people here knew that I had got home. Of course it was very kind of them to pay me so much attention, but you know, Dr. Ellesley, I value a friendly call like this infinitely more. Ceremony was always such a nuisance to me. *Do* take the easy chair now. Sister Dorothy Ann, dear, here is Dr. Ellesley, and I have persuaded him to stay and take a cup of tea with us. *Is* it not kind of him now, to come in and see us in such a charmingly friendly way? You know, I always say that I do so enjoy our friends coming in this way, it is so much more delightful than a ceremonious visit."

Miss Hacklebury shook hands with the Doctor, certainly more for his calling's sake than for his own this time. It was perfectly aggravating the way sister Waldemar had of twisting things about.

"Good afternoon, Doctor," she said, gathering up the stockings and thrusting them rather viciously into her work-basket. "I'm sure, sister Waldemar, if Dr. Ellesley means staying, I'm agreeable to it; and I hope I see you well, sir, after your visit to the Continent. Mr. Garton told us he had heard from you, and you were having a good time at Geneva, or some of those foreign places. Mr. Garton often used to come in and have a cup of tea with us, after he'd been teaching in the village; but, you see, I never made a bit of difference on his account, not looking at him in the light of a minister until he was ordained, and him not being accustomed to best china or anything of that sort at home, as I understood he wasn't. You know an ordained minister, as our poor dear father used to say, always made a difference. Yes, sister Waldemar, I'm going to fetch the china down directly, as soon as I've got the table cleared for tea."

And away went the matter-of fact Dorothy Ann to sort the pea-green cups and saucers, quickened thereto by a series of brisk telegraphic nods and signals from sister Waldemar, to whom Miss Hacklebury's extreme truthfulness was as inconvenient sometimes as that of her step-daughter Meta.

CHAPTER XIV.

"YOU must excuse my sister," said the solicitor's widow with an affectionate smile, when that excellent spinster's step was heard tramping upstairs towards the china closet. "She is so excessively matter-of-fact. Kind, you know, dear Dr. Ellesley, as kind as possible, but so *very* unpolished. I assure you it is quite an annoyance to me sometimes. Poor Mr. Waldemar used to say that no one, to look at us, would ever have the slightest idea that we were sisters; but then, as I said before, she is so admirably kind—indeed, she has been quite motherly to Mr. Garton since he took the little

Goverlies, because I told her that out of respect to you I should wish every attention paid to him. I knew you took such a very great interest in the young man."

Dr. Ellesley, after ineffectually commencing two or three sentences, succeeded in giving Mrs. Waldemar to understand that he appreciated the motive which had prompted her kindness to Mr. Garton. He did, he said, take a great interest in the young man, and hoped he would some day prove a credit to the college.

"But do you *know*," said Mrs. Waldemar, bending towards the Doctor, and dropping her voice gently to a confidential tone, Meta was away somewhere in the garden—"do you *know*, Doctor, I heard such a funny story about him the other day?—oh! such a *very* funny story. I cannot tell you how amused I was, though it gave me quite a little shock at first—you know I am so easily startled. And I was determined I would ask you about it as soon as *ever* I had the opportunity. They actually say, Dr. Ellesley, that his mother is a laundress somewhere in Millsmany. Ridiculous, isn't it. *Do* tell me now, if it is really so."

The Doctor could always find words to express himself when simple facts were required of him. And though he could not see anything remarkably funny in this particular fact, to account for Mrs. Waldemar's manner of introducing it, yet he began to tell her the truth, simply and straightforwardly.

"Yes; Mr. Garton's mother *does* occupy that position. She has earned her living in that way for the last twenty years. I do not see any necessity for mentioning the facts unless I am asked to do so, though I think it reflects infinite credit on the young man that he should have been able to attain to his present position."

"Oh! yes, yes, *indeed*," replied Mrs. Waldemar, following suit with admirable tact. "No one would think of anything but commending him for it. Indeed, I think myself it is quite charming. You know dear Mrs. Ellesley told me some time ago that he had had to struggle with adverse circumstances, but I never dreamed of a connection so romantic as that which was mentioned the other day. It is positively like one of the stories in that charming book, dear me! what is the name of that charming book about great men who have risen from the ranks? I really cannot remember the names of books, you know I am not a severe reader, my brain is so easily fatigued; but I know I was so *excessively* delighted with it. Then, Doctor, Mr. Garton really *has* nothing to depend upon but his own exertions."

" Nothing," said the Governor quietly, " but I have no doubt they will be quite sufficient for him, as his tastes are not expensive."

" And his mother?" suggested Mrs. Waldemar, " of course when she is no longer able to work, she will be dependent on him too."

" Yes. Stephen has always been a good lad to his mother. He will never let her want, so long as he can keep her in comfort."

" Dear me! how *charming!*" said Mrs. Waldemar, meditatively. She was not meditating on Stephen's filial affection though, as Dr. Ellesley might have supposed, but on the providential escape, for she could call it nothing less, which Meta had had. With that old woman dragging at him, Mr. Garton might wait years before he was able to settle. Unless he took her to live with him; and what young lady would tolerate such a mother-in-law."

" It is perfectly charming, Dr. Ellesley, to hear of such devotion. I really do not wonder now that you feel such an interest in the young man's welfare. I am sure he deserves *every* encouragement, *every* encouragement. And now *do* tell me how dear Mrs. Ellesley is? I am so naughty and forgetful not to have inquired after her before, but you see this affair of Mr. Garton's put everything else quite out of my thoughts. Is she *quite* well, and has she borne this distressingly hot weather with tolerable comfort? Dear old lady! I have thought about her so *very* often, because you know it is so very trying to elderly people, but *do* tell me now, that she is quite well."

Dr. Ellesley was not able to say that his mother was quite well. The hot summer really had enfeebled her, and for the last few weeks she had scarcely been able to walk beyond the College grounds. The Doctor therefore stated that fact in the brief succinct manner which characterised most of his statements of facts. It was only when circumstances forced him into the subjective vein that he was so painfully at a loss to make himself understood through the medium of well-chosen sentences.

Mrs. Waldemar's manner instantly changed from lively interest to the tenderest sympathy.

"Ah! I am *so* sorry. But do you know, Dr. Ellesley, for the last few months I have perceived a diminution of strength in your dear mother; so sensitive to changes in the weather and anything of that sort which young people like ourselves never feel at all. But age will tell, will it not, Dr. Ellesley?"

Dr. Ellesley replied that it would.

" Yes, and at your dear mother's advanced stage of life, you cannot, however much you might wish for it, expect to keep her with you very long. Not very long, you know, Dr. Ellesley. And she must feel the responsibilities of her position so much. Because a position like yours requires the lady who sustains it to be a good deal in company, receiving visitors, and dispensing social attentions, and other matters of that sort, which at your dear mother's advanced period of life *do*——"

At this point of the conversation Miss Hacklebury made her appearance, having one of the best damask tablecloths over her arm, followed by Buttons with the pea-green china.

"Dorothy Ann, dear," and Mrs. Waldemar looked imploringly towards her stiff, upright, exceedingly straightforward sister, "*are* you not distressed to hear that dear Mrs. Ellesley is not very well? She feels this hot weather so much. You remember I was only saying to you the other day that the weather is so very trying for persons who have begun to feel the touch of declining years. *Was* I not saying so, now?"

"Yes," said Miss Hacklebury, decisively, as she spread the damask cloth, Buttons standing by meanwhile with the china. "You were saying you felt it yourself very much, and I feel it too; people always do when they get past the prime of life like you and me"—Miss Hacklebury was feeling a little bit spiteful about the pea-green china, even yet. "And you see, Dr. Ellesley, your mother not being remarkably strong at the best of times, and you having so many strangers at the College, as Mr. Garton told us you had, it stands to reason she must be a little put about. Now, Buttons, set the tray down there, and then you can go. I can't have you fingering the china, or you'll chip some of the pieces, as sure as you're a girl."

Buttons retired, with a sidelong glance of reverence and wonder at the guest in whose honour such manifestations had been put forth. And Miss Hacklebury continued—

"You see, if I'd known you had been coming, I could have had the table set beforehand, not being a thing that I make a practice of doing when company is in the room, because sister Waldemar doesn't like it. But when people come on a sudden, it makes a difference, as I always say. But, however, you're very welcome. I have our dear father's respect for a minister. He always said a minister was an honour to his table, let him be a clergyman, or let him be what he might, and I feel just the same, and make them welcome to the best of everything I have."

Whereupon the Doctor began a sentence or two about a sense of obligation, but could not progress satisfactorily. He did manage though, to convey to Miss Hacklebury the impression that he felt her kindness.

"Oh! not a bit, Dr. Ellesley, not a bit. There isn't a person in Carriden-Regis I would have got that china down and dusted it for with more pleasure than yourself. And I'm sure I wish Mrs. Ellesley could have come with you, if it hadn't been that she is only enjoying poor health at the present. But it's the extra company that's trying her, that's just what it is. You see at her time of life people can't bear to be put about as they can when their age don't sit so heavily upon them. I *do* wonder, Dr. Ellesley,"

And Dorothy Ann paused as she was setting the cups and saucers round the tray, and looked the Doctor straight in the face, as innocently as though she had been asking him whether he would take muffin or crumpet.

"I *do* wonder, Dr. Ellesley, you never think of getting married. It would be so much more comfortable for you."

"Dorothy *Ann*, dear! Dorothy *Ann*, dear!" and Mrs. Waldemar attempted to blush, but did not succeed to any appreciable extent. "How *can* you think of such a thing? And to mention it too in the presence of Dr. Ellesley. I *am* so surprised at you."

"Why?" said Dorothy Ann, looking unconcerned. "I don't see anything improper in it. And as for mentioning it in Dr. Ellesley's presence, I should think he's the very man whose presence it ought to be mentioned in. And I am sure I have thought very often what a wonder it is he doesn't think of getting married."

The Doctor looked at Miss Hacklebury, and then at the pea-green china, and then at Mrs. Waldemar, who appeared so excessively shocked at her sister's rudeness in mentioning such a thing, that she was almost on the point of giving way; and then, folding his hands quietly, he said,

"I—I *have* been thinking about it, Miss Hacklebury."

Sister Waldemar began to count the

stitches in her embroidery, and being of opinion that at this juncture of affairs a little
private conversation would be desirable, murmured—

"Dorothy Ann, dear, *will* you go and see
where darling Meta is?"

Just the very thing Dr. Ellesley wished she
had done half an hour ago.

CHAPTER XV.

THAT same evening—the evening after the examination—Stephen Garton sat in his study, utterly spent and weary with the hard mental strain of the previous day. The examination had lasted eight hours. It was partly oral, partly by questions proposed at their own option by the different professors, and to be replied to in writing. No books were allowed, no references of any kind, and the six competitors were placed at a distance from each other, that mutual help or consultation might be impossible. When a sufficient number of questions had been proposed in the different subjects of examination, and

the time allowed for their ˙solution had ex-
pired, the competition was declared to be at
an end. The written replies of each student,
duly folded, sealed, and attested by the student's name, attached in a blank envelope,
were given in charge of the professors, who
assembled next morning to look them over,
and pronounce judgment.

A clear day had to elapse before the announcement of the successful candidate, and
this day Stephen Garton was spending in
his study. Spending it in utter idleness, for
that eight hours' spell of competition, to say
nothing of the almost intolerable anxiety and
suspense of the interval which had to be
spent in uncertainty as to the result of the
examination, kept him from any further exertion either of mind or body. Time after time
the College clock had marked off the hours
all through that dreary, fateful day, whilst

the professors were closeted in one of the lecture-rooms, deciding who was to be presented next morning with the Burton medal; until now the early autumn twilight had begun to darken Stephen's little den—that dingy, scantily-furnished study, where, in the years past, he had done so much hard work, and laid up such store of mental wealth.

Would he have to toil there any more? Would to-morrow open the gate for him to a new, wider, brighter life? Would it give him what he had been looking forward to so long—independence, and a good standing-place in the world? Would it not only set him out of reach of the galling pressure of poverty, but give him even more than wealth, —honour, name, position; and in giving these, give him also the right to reach out and clasp for his own, in the sight of all the world, that treasure of Meta's love, which as

yet he had only dared to look upon in secret? Or would it bid him back again to
the old narrow groove of toil and patience
and self-denial? Would the bright shining
of another's sun leave him in darkness?
Must that success, which would have been so
dearly prized by him, go to another, who,
even if he prized it, could not need it half
so much?

Stephen did not know. He could not tell.
He dared not even pray, as some good men
might have prayed, that the morrow would
bring him success. For as the joy of another in this thing could only be purchased
at the expense of his own, so that
which he so greatly longed for, if given
to him, must be taken from one who had
toiled for it as hardly, and coveted it as
eagerly, though not with the same motive,
as himself. He could only ask that, having

done his duty as far as he knew it, he might be able to wait patiently for the result; and that whether such result was success or disappointment, he might at least not miss the strength which duty done will always bring to those who do it faithfully.

And yet, if only the coming day might bring him success! Stephen Garton felt such a sickening sense of dread when he thought that it could bring him anything else. For so much depended upon that success. It would be not merely the fulfilling of an idle vanity, the gratification of a selfish desire for notoriety, but it would give him that which he had been toiling for so long and so painfully—that which, without it, would still be removed years and years away from him; the ability to place his mother beyond the reach of want, and to win for himself the woman whom he had chosen out of all the

world to be his wife. Sometimes he thought
he must triumph. He had worked so very
hard for success; it would do so much for
him, so much more than it could do for any
of the others.   What did Rodney Charnock,
with his millionaire uncle and his splendid
prospects, or Banks, who was going to be
an independent gentleman, or Fensley, who
had friends and patronage at command, care
for a few hundred pounds and a free college
course, and what were honours to them compared to the gain that he could reap from
them? They had enough and to spare already of all that life could give; he had so
little, and for that little he had toiled so
hard.   Surely they could better bear than
he could the sadness and bitterness of disappointment.

And then he pictured to himself what he
would do if the Burton medal really was

awarded to him. First of all, he would go
to his mother and tell her the good news;
have her away from that mean little home
where she had struggled through so many
painful years, to one where she could rest
and be quiet for the remainder of her days.
And then he would seek Meta, dear little
Meta, who he knew would be waiting so an-
xiously for him, though she never said a
word, and tried so hard to seem as though
she did not care very much about it. And
he would tell her, not a mean man now,
nor poor any longer, what for his poverty
and his meanness had been left unspoken so
long between them; how through all those
long weeks of toil the hope of her love had
cheered him, and how he only cared for this
honour, that having it, he might be more
worthy of her. And almost as he sat there
in his dingy study, amongst the creeping

shadows of the autumn twilight, he could see her quick look of joy, hear her speak what need now no longer be left untold, and feel her lips touching his for the kiss which, save in some sweet fancy, he had never dared to place there yet.

It was so much easier to think of all this, to dream happy dreams of love and home and honour, than to turn to the other side of the picture, and think what life would be if another carried away the prize which he hoped to win. If Rodney Charnock conquered and he lost. Then he thought of that evening, four months ago, when he helped Charnock, when he had put in his enemy's way what might tend to his own defeat. He almost wondered how he could have done it. But he had no Meta's love to toil for, and hope for, then. It would have cost him so little, so very little then, to lose the scholarship, compared to the great dark cloud which would come up over his life now, if what he had been toiling for so long was dashed away from him. Then he only worked for duty, now he worked for love. Perhaps his poor old mother, saying her prayers, and meditating on her spiritual experience in that brick-floored cottage down one of the back streets of Millsmany, would have felt a pang deeper than Stephen had ever caused her before, could she have known that the love which for so many years she had borne to him, stirred him less now, than the thought of this young girl whose name as yet was unspoken, save in the stillness of his own heart. But old Mrs. Garton had that mother's sorrow to come, and she would have to bear it as most mothers do, patiently and silently.

Whilst Stephen was thinking over all these

things, one of the wardens came up the cor-
ridor with the evening letters. There were
two for Mr. Garton. One was from Mrs.
Waldemar. He knew the delicate, angular
handwriting on the envelope, for she had
written to him once before, a very friendly
affectionate note, requesting his presence at
Percy Cottage to converse with him respecting some private teaching to which she
wished to introduce him. The other was
from Mrs. Goverly. It was very brief, and
ran thus:—

"Mrs. Goverly presents her compliments
to Mr. Garton, and begs to say, that in consequence of certain unpleasant statements
which have come to her knowledge respecting his position and connections, she is
under the painful necessity of requesting
him to discontinue his attendance at Ivy
Lodge."

Stephen threw that on one side, and broke the seal of Mrs. Waldemar's letter. It was longer, and, like the one which he had received from her before, underlined at almost every word.

"Mrs. Waldemar begs to inform Mr. Gar-·ton that, in consequence of facts which have been made known to her, and which she has since ascertained to be perfectly correct, she feels herself compelled to relinquish the intercourse which has hitherto subsisted between Mr. Garton and her own family. Mrs. Waldemar feels excessively annoyed at Mr. Garton's unparalleled impertinence, for she can call it by no other name, in having presumed to thrust himself upon the hospitalities of a family infinitely above him in social position, and who would never have felt themselves justified in offering him any attention whatever, had they been acquainted, as Mr. Garton ought to have acquainted them at the outset, with the extreme vulgarity of his antecedents. [Mrs. Waldemar desires that Mr. Garton's only reply to this communication shall be his obedience to the request which it conveys, neither herself nor any member of her family desiring further intercourse with a person who has already proved himself so wanting in honourable frankness."

That note had cost Mrs. Waldemar at least an hour's severe study, and frequent references to the polite letter writer, before it was finished to her complete satisfaction. Because, after all, she was not really dismissing Mr. Garton from the privilege of a visiting acquaintance with her own family on account of anything she had heard respecting his connections at Millsmany, but because she felt there was danger in his intercourse with

Meta, and **Mr.** Charnock would be so much more advantageous a match for her stepdaughter. Nothing could be urged against him as an excuse for what she was now doing, except the fact of his humble belongings; and yet, after having almost in their first interview professed herself acquainted with his history, and made his early difficulties a plea for the interest which she manifested in him, it would be rather awkward now to make that very history and those very difficulties her pretext for dismissing him from an intimacy which she had been the first to foster.

· That was why she desired him not to intrude upon her for the purpose of a personal interview; a privilege which he might very naturally claim, for the sake of some further explanation. An explanation was the very thing she wished to avoid, for she feared being able to justify herself in it. She had seen enough of him to feel sure that his pride would keep him away after such a note as that. And in the event of his not securing that Burton prize, and so having to remain at the College for some time longer, a complete cessation of his visits under present circumstances was an end that must be accomplished by any means. Therefore, on the whole, she thought she had done what needed to be done very effectually. If he went away to Germany, it would be all right; if he staid, Meta would be as safe now as though she had never seen him.

After she had written the note she put on her bonnet and went across the green to Mrs. Goverly, who was prepared for her visit by the note which Buttons had taken on the preceding evening. And she so represented to the solicitor's wife the state of affairs, and so urged upon her, for the sake of her children, the advisability, not to say positive duty, of removing them from the care of a person whose antecedents so utterly disqualified him for so serious a charge, that Mrs. Goverly, who never thought of such a thing as acting upon her own responsibility, wrote there and then, at the dictation of her lady-patroness, the note which, in company with Mrs. Waldemar's, reached Stephen Garton the night after the examination.

Stephen read them both several times over. Then he leaned his arms upon the deal table, laid his head upon them, and fell to thinking. He was sitting there when the September moon rose over the Carriden-Regis hills, and began to silver the bare walls of his little room. He was sitting there when that September moon sank behind the brown Millsmany moors. He was still sitting there when the first red streaks of sunrise woke the linnets to their matin song, and he had not yet stirred when the great bell of the College, sounding the hour of seven, roused the students, and bade them prepare for that day which, to one of them at least, would be a day of triumph.

Stephen felt, as he prepared to obey its summons, that he could bear to lose the Burton scholarship now.

CHAPTER XVI.

IF it was a day of triumph but to one of the students, it was a day of excitement to them all. Coming only once in four years, it was welcomed with a due amount of ceremony. The awarding of the prize took place in the common hall, which was decorated for the occasion with flowers and evergreens from the College grounds, and on this bright September morning it was gay with many a wreath and festoon hung from beam to beam of the oaken roof. At the end where the Governor's Plato used to stand, a platform was erected for the examining Professors and

those connected with the College. The
audience was not confined to the students,
but all who could obtain cards of invitation from the Professors were admitted, as
well as the friends of the students; and as
these were chiefly ladies, their presence did
more towards the decoration of the hall, as
some of the speakers used gallantly to ob-
serve, than even the evergreens and gor-
geously-tinted autumn flowers, which were
lavished with such profusion around.

Rodney Charnock had obtained the consent
of Mrs. Waldemar to place herself and Meta
under his care for the occasion. Rodney had
certainly lost no opportunity of following up
the advantage which that first visit gave
him. He was continually dropping in now
as if by accident, at Percy Cottage, with
some message from his sister for Meta or
Mrs. Waldemar. Sometimes it was a book to

lend, sometimes one to borrow; sometimes a new song which he fancied would suit Miss Waldemar's voice, sometimes a fern which he should be so delighted if Mrs. Waldemar would accept for the little Wardian case which stood in the bay window of the dining-room. At last scarcely a day passed without some civility of this kind, which, as Rodney Charnock intended should be the case, placed him upon a footing of intimacy far more than equal to anything which had ever been granted to Mr. Garton.

Miss Hacklebury did not draw to him very much, particularly as sister Waldemar insisted that, as he was quite the gentleman, the silver cake-basket and the best teapot, not to say the pea-green china, should be put into requisition whenever he came in about tea-time. Miss Hacklebury did not profess to have great discernment of character, but she always knew when she could get on with anyone, and she felt from the very first that she should never be able to get on with Mr. Charnock. He said too many pretty things of people present, and too many ugly ones of people absent, for her to have much faith in him; and she had a shrewd notion that when she and sister Waldemar were the people absent, they would fare no better than others.

She rather looked forward to Stephen Garton coming back to the Cottage again, when the little Goverlies had returned from the sea-side, and the fuss of this examination was over. For Mrs. Waldemar, with the reticence of true wisdom, had abstained from telling sister Dorothy Ann anything about that letter to Stephen, and had also cautioned Mrs. Goverly, with what appeared to that easily-managed lady a beautiful exercise of Christian charity, against further injuring the young man by exposing the extremely humiliating circumstances of his former life.

Miss Hacklebury rather looked forward then to Stephen's return, when that examination was done with. Unless, indeed, he got the scholarship, which she began to think would be rather a questionable advantage to him; if, as she was quite sure was the case, he and Meta were becoming attached to each other. Meta never said anything; she was a very shy, quiet little creature, but sometimes, when Stephen Garton, coming to sit with them for an hour or two in an evening, as he so often did when sister Waldemar was away, began to speak about the possibility of his gaining this prize, and what a fine thing it would be for him to go to Germany for the winter session, she had noticed that Meta, though she tried very hard to appear as if nothing was ·the matter, turned pale and looked troubled; and once or twice, after Stephen had gone away, seemed almost ready to cry. If Stephen *did* set off to Germany without saying anything to Meta, Miss Hacklebury knew it would be a dreary winter for the poor girl. Because, though young Garton had none of those nice little attentive ways about him which made sister Waldemar praise Mr. Charnock up to the very skies, yet it was plain enough what he thought about Meta, and if he had never said it out in words, he had in looks, which meant just the same thing.

Supposing, then, he did not get this scholarship, he would just go studying on at the College as usual, coming into the village once or twice a week for his private teaching; and then of course he would begin to drop in again as he did before the little Goverlies went away to the sea-side; and perhaps by-and-by he and Meta would understand each other. Dorothy Ann did not think sister Waldemar would greatly object to her step-daughter becoming engaged. Indeed, she had said more than once how glad she should be to get her off her hands. And though of course Mr. Garton would not be able to marry just yet, still Meta was only young, and could afford to wait. And she was just the sort of quiet little girl, too, who would not aspire to anything brilliant. She did not think a better lot could fall to her than that she should become Stephen Garton's be-trothed, and wait for him three or four years; just as *she* had once thought to wait for *her* Stephen, long ago. It did not seem a weary waiting to her then; it would not seem weary to Meta, now.

Miss Hacklebury thought it was most likely

the idea of Mr. Garton going away to Germany which had made Meta look rather sad
for the last few days. She seemed to have
lost her light springy ways, and if there
was a knock at the door she would start
so nervously, almost as nervously as sister
Waldemar; and such a dreary, disappointed
expression came over her face when Buttons,
opening the sitting-room door, announced
Mr. Charnock, with his flatteries and his
compliments and his nonsense. Poor little
Meta! Miss Hacklebury hoped very much
that Stephen Garton would not go to Germany; or that if he *did* go, he would come
to some sort of understanding with Meta before he went.

But if sister Dorothy Ann did not get
on very well with Mr. Charnock, Mrs. Waldemar more than made up for any little
deficiency in that direction by the unfailing

courtesy which she lavished upon her new friend, and the unbounded hospitality with which she pressed him to come in whenever he chose. Rodney Charnock was not slow to avail himself of the privilege. He did not as yet know whether he cared enough about Meta to come to anything definite with her, but at anyrate she was a downright pleasant little plaything to trifle with; so innocent and unsuspecting and simple, such a delightful contrast to the generality of his female acquaintance. And the very unconsciousness with which she received his attentions, not seeming indeed to know that they were attentions, was enough to make him offer them with redoubled assiduity. Here was something at last to conquer. He had never caused her to blush with gratified vanity yet. Say what he might, flatter her as he would, she just used to look at him with that quaint, serious look. It was positively charming. He had never had such a zest in making himself agreeable before.

And then there was that fellow Garton to triumph over. It would be altogether too much for a charity student to win the Burton prize and the Waldemar prize too. If Garton's brains secured the one, as everybody in the College said they would, Charnock was determined that his own sweet words should secure the other; at any rate, seem to secure it. Whether he chose to keep it or not, was quite another question.

That was why he pressed his services so earnestly upon Mrs. Waldemar on the occasion of this gathering in the College. Sitting side by side with Meta in that brilliant hall, or strolling about the grounds afterwards, with her leaning on his arm, her sweet face downcast perhaps for some tender speech of his, Rodney Charnock thought he could convince the charity student, even in the very moment of his victory, supposing it came to a victory, that he had not won all that might have been won, and even that in straining every nerve to carry off one prize, he had allowed another, still more valuable, to slip through his fingers.

By noon the common hall was filled. Upon the platform were gathered the professors belonging to the Carriden-Regis and other colleges; some of them wizened and frumpy, like the old divine who had slipped away three or four years ago, for Dr. Ellesley to take his place; some grand, scholarly-looking men, with brows that seemed to be toppling over with the weight of intellect that sat enthroned upon them; some hale, jolly divines, with a suggestive circularity of waistcoat and a genial twinkle in their eyes, which looked as if it might have something to do with old port; others lean and shrivelled, as though the mind within them had devoured the matter without, except so much of it as was absolutely necessary for the daily purposes of life. In the midst of them sat the Governor, whose it was to award the prize. He bore himself with grave, quiet dignity, chatting now and then to one and another of the professors, without a vestige of the nervous embarrassment which clung about him in ordinary social life. Here he was in his own place. He knew what was required of him, and he did it like a man.

The rest of the hall was thronged with ladies and students, the resplendent toilettes of the one contrasting ✦ effectively with the sombre garb of the other. In a very conspicuous place sat **Mrs.** Waldemar and her step-daughter, with Rodney Charnock between them, paying such attention to each in her turn as the time and the place would allow.

Mrs. Waldemar was a woman who could keep almost any number of gentlemen employed in waiting upon her. Indeed, she never seemed **to** be quite content unless someone **was** doing something for her. Her vinaigrette wanted opening, **or** her scent-bottle had got **out of** order, as it always did when she took it into public, or she dropped her handkerchief, **or** she wanted her bouquet holding whilst she fastened her glove; **or** a window near her **must** be opened, **for** she thought she should really be obliged **to** give way unless she could have a little fresh air, **or** the same **must** be closed, lest a cold blast should bring on neuralgia.

So that Mr. Rodney, as he danced attendance upon her, and fulfilled, one after another, all her feminine behests, did not feel that he occupied his post for nothing, more especially as he had selected a position where Stephen Garton, who was sitting on one of the side benches, with no galaxy of fair ladies about him, could not fail, if he turned his eyes in that direction, to see the whole performance.

The Governor opened the proceedings with a short speech, strangely unlike his halting, spasmodic attempts in the Percy Cottage drawing-room. This was clear, concise, compact; every word well chosen, well placed; no beginning of sentences two or three times before they could be made to run alone, no painful straggling of the words into helpless confusion towards the close. With as little useless verbiage as possible, he said what he had to say, but said it with a purpose and definiteness which fixed it for ever in the memories of those who had intellect enough to understand it.

Mrs. Waldemar leaned forward with eager interest when the Doctor began to speak, her dark eyes beaming, her face wreathed into fascinating smiles. Had Dr. Ellesley been careering triumphantly through one of the most splendid perorations of modern pulpit eloquence, set as thickly with trope and metaphor and allegory and illustration, as an Indian prince's robes of state with rubies and diamonds, Mrs. Waldemar could not have followed him with more apparently rapt admiration than she manifested, as, in those few short, severely simple sentences, he set forth the conditions of the award, the subjects of study which it involved, and the objects for which the scholarship had been founded.

" So grand! so *sublime!*" murmured Mrs. Waldemar to her attendant squire. " I do so *dote* upon talent, it is such a splendid thing, is it not?"

Rodney Charnock quizzed the Governor through his eye-glass, and then said that talent was a tolerably handy thing in its way, and convenient for getting a fellow on in the world, particularly when he had neither family nor fortune to back him up. But for the rest, he thought those extremely talented people were rather a bore.

" Oh! certainly," said Mrs. Waldemar, her thoughts reverting at once to Stephen Garton, who sat on the opposite side, moody, abstracted, apparently paying little heed to the Governor or his speech. " I don't for one moment place it in competition with

birth and breeding, and a good social position. A good position, you know, Mr. Charnock, is *everything.* I should never think of
tolerating a man unless I knew he was
everything that could be desired in that respect. My vinaigrette, please, thank you;
and oh! if that window *could* be opened
just a very little bit, Mr. Charnock, it
would he *such* a relief to me. I declare I
am positively gasping for breath, and the
Governor's speech has excited me so.
You know I am so foolish when I hear
anything really impressive. Just a very little bit, if you please, or I shall take cold
from the draught."

Rodney jumped up and opened the window, in return for which attention Mrs. Waldemar rewarded him with one of her sweetest smiles. She did so enjoy a little public
homage of this kind. And then she gave

him her bouquet to hold, whilst she arranged her bonnet strings.

When the Governor's address was concluded, the professors followed with their speeches of various degrees of interest. The gentleman with the large circularity of waistcoat made a profound impression upon the audience by his remarks on self-denial, and the ruggedness of the upward path to fame, and the noble resolve with which, if he would one day reach its loftiest elevation, the student must spurn all allurements of ease and luxury, and the more than Spartan fortitude with which he must look down on the mere gratifications of flesh and sense. A train of remarks which was responded to with a vast amount of cheering from all parts of the building, such an amount that the circular gentleman resolved to uphold self-denial and Spartan frugality on the platform for ever.

Last of all, when everything had been said that needed to be said, and perhaps a great deal more; when the successful student, whoever he might chance to be, had been patted on the back and bidden not to be over-proud of his laurels, and when those who might be unsuccessful had been encouraged to take heart and comfort themselves with the reflection—sorry comfort most likely, when the time came for it— that, though worsted in the present strife, they had at least, like the athlete in the old Greek and Roman games, gained strength for life by the training which their preparation had involved; and when the rest of the young men had been urged to profit by the noble example of energy and perseverance which the competitors had displayed, Dr. Ellesley rose, and taking from a case on the table before him the gold medal of the

Burton scholarship, with the various certificates belonging to it, asked the chief examining professor for the name of the successful student.

The professor handed him a folded paper, from which Dr. Ellesley read as follows:—

"After carefully examining the papers laid before us, and weighing their respective merits, we, the undersigned professors and examiners appointed by the College of Carriden-Regis, in pursuance of the directions of the late Jonas Burton, award the gold medal, with all rights and privileges pertaining thereto, to Stephen Garton."

CHAPTER XVII.

THIS announcement was followed by a great tumult of clapping and cheering, in the midst of which Stephen Garton, not looking quite so triumphant as some of the people expected he would look, came forward to receive his certificates.

But then, as the professors remarked one to another, the immense amount of toil and study which the competition must have involved to a young man of his somewhat slow and heavy type of intellect, would produce a considerable effect upon his spirits, and the intense anxiety, which of course he could not help feeling, even after the strain of mental

effort was over, before the award was decided, might naturally be expected to have
its effect upon his behaviour. Apparently
he was not one of those young men, they
said, who can be excited over anything.
Most likely, if he had lost the prize, he
would have been just as outwardly calm
about it. And even if at other times he
could have got up a little enthusiasm, it was
often the case that after a struggle like this,
the successful competitor in the moment of
victory felt his triumph less than those who
witnessed it.

"Dreadfully plain, is he not?" said Belle
Charnock, turning the mass of feathers
and lace which she called her bonnet, towards a young lady, equally fashionable, but
not equally *prononcé*, by her side. "Dreadfully plain, isn't he, and so awkward in his
manners?"

"Oh! dear, now, how *can* you say so?" replied the young lady friend enthusiastically. "I do so adore a plain man—distinctively plain, you know; and I call his manners perfect—just the thing for a literary person. One always looks for something a little out of the common way in a literary man. Oh, I *do* think he is splendid! I declare I am perfectly in love with him. He is *so* distinguished."

Belle Charnock laughed.

"Splendidly distinguished! His mother is quite a low person, takes in washing, and lives in a back yard in Millsmany. Father used to be a disreputable sort of fellow—weaver, or something of that sort."

"Oh, indeed!" replied the young lady, not at all enthusiastically, "that alters the case."

And nothing more was said about Stephen's distinctive plainness.

Rodney Charnock clapped as energetically as anyone.

"Very glad for him, poor fellow!" he said, loudly enough for those around him to hear, as he threw himself carelessly back in his seat; and then with an air of easy familiarity leaned towards Meta, and began to toy with the flowers in her bouquet. Stephen could see him do it plainly enough from the elevated position where he was standing on the platform now amongst the professors.

"Very glad he has come off first. You know, a great many of our fellows, when they heard he was going in for it, did not think it gentlemanly to compete with him, because a little money would be everything in the world to him, dependent as he has been on charity ever since he came to the College. I'm very glad for him, 'pon my word I am."

"Pray what do *you* think of it, Miss Waldemar?" he continued, looking tenderly down into Meta's face.

But Meta only answered very quietly,

"I suppose it is all right."

Mrs. Waldemar thought her step-daughter might be a little disappointed that Mr. Charnock had not got the prize. Such marked attentions as he had been paying to her for the last week or two could not fail to create a feeling of affection towards him on her part, and lead her to hope for his success. Rodney Charnock's self-love, too, prompted him to the same conclusion, and with the eagerness of a suitor who feels himself favoured, he hastened to assure her that there was not the slightest need for sympathy, so far as he was concerned.

"Don't think about me for a moment, Miss Waldemar. I assure you I could have taken it as easily as not if I had gone in for it regularly from the first, but I thought it was only fair to give the poor fellow a chance. Poverty and low breeding and all that sort of thing keeps a fellow down so, you know, if he doesn't get a lift like this once in a while. And then," continued Rodney with a glance of impressive tenderness towards the unconscious Meta, "the Burton scholarship is not the only prize which a Carriden-Regis student may hope to win."

Whether Meta's vanity enabled her to take in the full meaning of this speech is uncertain. Mrs. Waldemar understood it, however, and the bland smile with which she favoured Mr. Charnock at its conclusion was a sufficient intimation that he might count upon her best wishes and her most favourable offices in the winning of *that* prize.

After the award of the scholarship the proceedings terminated. Most of the students turned out with their lady friends into the College grounds, and sauntering through the shrubberies, chatted over the affair of the day. Stephen stayed behind with the Governor, to have his certificates duly signed. There was not much time for quiet thinking over anything that had happened, for he .was beset as soon as the audience broke up with congratulations—professors coming to shake hands with him, students bringing their friends to be introduced, bevies of fair ladies swarming round him with fine speeches and pretty compliments. All of which Stephen received very quietly. The one word ·of praise which would have sounded so sweet from Meta's lips was left unspoken, and that being wanting, the rest were little worth.

He did see her once, though, during the day. Most of the company had left the grounds. Only a few scattered groups lingered as the afternoon wore on. Stephen was coming down the beech-tree avenue —not coming alone, for the Burton prizeman never lacked friends to cluster round him on the day of triumph—and before he was aware of it, he encountered Mrs. Waldemar, Rodney Charnock, and Meta.

She was leaning on Charnock's arm. He was evidently talking some pretty nonsense to her, for her eyes were towards the ground, and there was a flush, not exactly of pleasure, but of conscious embarrassment, on her face. Mrs. Waldemar, on the other side of Meta, was chatting away with her customary bright impulsiveness. As they met Stephen, however, she drew herself up with an air of supreme indifference, and walked past without condescending a single glance towards him. Meta kept her eyes upon the ground. Rodney Charnock's patronizing nod as they passed seemed to say,

"Glad you have got a lift, old boy!"

And Stephen thought he heard him remark immediately after,

"Time he took his mother out of that back yard."

It was little consequence now, though, what anyone said about him. The hardest thrust had been given, the worst pain endured. Meta had lost faith in him, had given him up for this pompous young dangler. If his triumph that day had been purchased at the expense of a little disappointment to others, that disappointment had been bitterly overbalanced by the victory of another for which his own life had been wrecked.

The proceedings of the day were wound up by a dinner given in the evening in honour of the Burton prizeman; a ponderous, stately affair, where Stephen's health was drunk, and he was expected to reply in a lengthy speech, marked by the brilliance and vivacity which success might be supposed to have produced in his feelings. Then followed other healths and speeches, all drunk and responded to with more or less enthusiasm; and finally three good ringing cheers from the assembled students, and those of the Professors who had not quite outlived their youthful hilarity; after which the successful competitor was allowed to retire, and betake himself to such repose as was likely to follow in the wake of so much excitement.

A permission which Stephen received very thankfully, and with not half the amount of smiling triumph which the students thought he ought to have manifested on the occasion.

There is no need to follow him into that mean dingy little room, where for another night he kept his solitary vigil. What he had toiled for so long was given at last, honour, competence, room to work and make for himself a good name in the world. But finding the room to work, he had lost the heart to use it, and winning the good name, there was no longer anyone to share it with him. He had struggled through a long dark night to the morning dawn, but when it came his eyes were dim, so that he could no more see its brightness. The darkness and the light were both alike to him now.

So often, upon the hands which have many a time been outstretched for it, God lays, when they no longer care to hold it, the gift which once they so eagerly coveted to grasp; and crowns with long-wished-for laurels the brow which can only wear them, when given, with weariness and pain.

END OF THE SECOND VOLUME.

LONDON: PRINTED BY MACDONALD AND TUGWELL, BLENHEIM HOUSE.